Kit was ~~...~~

than she ~~...~~

Especially to this man who'd just kissed her.

"Admit it, Kit," Reese said. "That hard shell of yours cracked. Maybe I should have peeled it away layer by layer."

"Better men than you have tried." She turned to face him, regaining enough composure to battle him.

"Bold words," Reese said, a knowing glitter in his eyes. "And lies. I tasted the inexperience on your lips. I doubt if your experience goes beyond a few kisses behind the barn. I'd swear you never made it to the hayloft."

"Is that something I should be ashamed about?" Kit challenged.

"No, on the contrary." Lazily Reese reached out, his fingers closing around the shirt button nestled in the vee of her breasts. "Every man likes to be the first."

Janet Dailey
Americana

LORD OF THE HIGH LONESOME

Harlequin Books

TORONTO • NEW YORK • LONDON
AMSTERDAM • PARIS • SYDNEY • HAMBURG
STOCKHOLM • ATHENS • TOKYO • MILAN

The state flower depicted on the cover of this book is
prairie rose.

Janet Dailey Americana edition published October 1987
Second printing September 1988
Third printing September 1989

ISBN 373-21934-2

Harlequin Presents edition published June 1980
Second printing February 1982

Original hardcover edition published in 1980
by Mills & Boon Limited

CHAPTER ONE

WINTER-GRAY CLOUDS darkened the afternoon sky, the temperature chilling, a cold wind whistling. Kit Bonner waded through a fresh snowdrift the wind had piled on the path to the door. On the stoop, she paused to stomp the snow from her boots, her brown eyes scanning the bleak Dakota landscape beyond the living snow fence of trees.

The cold turned her breath into a puffy white vapor and reddened her cheeks and the tip of her nose. Her lips seemed frozen, incapable of movement without splitting. A creeping numbness was spreading through her limbs despite the long, thermal underwear beneath her denims and the fleece-lined parka.

Yet Kit didn't hurry into the promised warmth of the house perched on the slope of a hill. Her attention was on the threatening darkness of the sky, her mind wondering how severe this winter storm would be and how well the cattle on the range would weather it.

A horse whinnied up by the barns, swinging her gaze in its direction. A shaggy-coated bay had its head over the corral fence, its ears pricked toward the outer barn door. Lew Simpson, one of the ranch hands, had just closed the door and was walking away, his Stetsoned head bent down, his body leaning into the wind. His destination was the old bunkhouse where friendly, welcoming smoke curled from its chimney.

Unconsciously Kit's gaze continued its arc until it was stopped by the imposing structure of the main ranch house. For as long as Kit could remember it had been referred to as the Big House. From atop the hill it commanded a sweeping view of the ranch buildings and the rugged North Dakota landscape. No smoke came from its chimneys nor any light from its windows. It stood empty, its doors and windows locked and shuttered.

The sight of it set her teeth on edge, thinning her lips and pressing them tightly closed. With an abrupt turn, Kit reached for the door and yanked it open to stride inside, slamming the door, peeling off her thickly lined leather gloves with jerky movements.

"Is that you, Kitty?" A voice called from the living room just beyond the small kitchen.

"Yes." She unwrapped the woolen scarf that was wound around her neck and over the faded Stetson hat atop her head.

Heavy footsteps entered the kitchen. "Just heard on the radio that they're issuing stockmen's warnings."

"Yes, I know." Kit didn't bother to glance at her grandfather as she draped the scarf over a coat hook and began unbuttoning her parka. "I talked to Sam McKenna today and made arrangements to airdrop some hay to the stock Lew and Frank can't reach by snowmobile." There was a husky quality to her voice, a sound that could have been pleasant if the words hadn't been issued so gruffly. "I was hoping we'd get a chinook before the next blizzard came."

"If wishes were horses—"

"Yes, I know, Nate." The parka joined the scarf on the hook as Kit impatiently cut in on her grandfather's recitation of the old adage.

There was a second's pause before he asked, "Did you get the mail?" with no reprimand for her curtness.

It was unnecessary since a twinge of conscience took any edge from her reply. "It's in my coat pocket."

With a hand braced against the wall for balance, Kit slipped a snow-covered heel into the bootjack. Her peripheral vision saw his arm reaching for her parka and the mail peeking out of its pocket.

"Anything special in it?"

"It looked like mostly junk mail and a couple of magazines," she answered, taking the boots she had removed and setting them on the newspapers next to the wall.

"At least we'll have something to read if we're snowed in." With the mail in hand, Nate Bonner turned to walk through the kitchen to the living room.

His philosophic attitude grated. Kit knew there was little that could be done except wait out the storm, but youth was seldom granted the wisdom of age to know the difference between the things that can be changed and those that can't. It was all there in the irritated glance she tossed at his departing back, shoulders faintly stooped with age, legs permanently bowed, and a thatch of snow-white hair on his head.

The impulse to protest his calm acceptance of the situation was stifled as Kit noticed the lack of spring to his step. Nothing would be served by giving rein to her short temper. Besides, he wasn't to blame for the leftover irritation coursing through her.

"Is there any coffee hot?" she questioned instead.

The faded brown Stetson was the last of her outer garments to be removed. It loosed a cascading tangle of chestnut gold hair that had been tucked inside its crown. It tumbled around her shoulders, a glistening contrast to the red and black plaid of the man's flannel shirt Kit wore, one of many in her winter wardrobe, like the men's cotton shirts that dominated her summer wear.

The rare times that her male attire was questioned, Kit claimed she wore it because men's things were cheaper and longer lasting. But it was part of a hard, protective shell, like her brown eyes that never let anyone see in and the always proud and defensive tilt of her chin.

"Coffee's on the stove."

In stocking feet Kit dodged the puddles of melting snow, stepping out of the narrow lobby into the kitchen. She walked to the gas stove, which, like the rest of the small house and its furnishings, bordered on being antique. An almost equally old, metal percolater sat on a burner. Kit touched its side with her fingers to be sure its contents were still hot before opening the cupboard door beside the stove.

"Do you want a cup, Nate?" she called.

There was an instant of silence before he answered with a rather absent, "No, thanks."

Bypassing the china cups and saucers on the shelf, Kit took out an old ironstone mug. A fine film of dust covered the china. It hadn't been used, except to be moved and cleaned during Kit's rare housecleaning spates, in the four years since her grandmother died.

Her grandfather had gone steadily downhill since then, losing his vigor, his drive. Nate Bonner had always seemed ageless to Kit, but she had watched him grow old. He had become merely the figurehead of the Flying Eagle Ranch that had once flourished under his management. Kit was the one who now gave the orders and made sure they were carried out.

No one had disputed her right to take over, not because she was a woman and not because she was young, having turned twenty-one this past fall. Everyone accepted it as being just and fair under the circumstances.

In the living room her grandfather sat in an old-fashioned wing-backed chair. His head was tipped back to peer through the lower half of the reading glasses perched on his nose. A reading lamp on the table beside him cast a circle of light onto the letter in his hand, the rest of the day's mail lying on his lap.

A matching chair to the one he sat in flanked the other side of the table, its maroon cushions worn almost threadbare in spots. With her steaming coffee mug in hand Kit walked to it. Her grandmother had always sat there and Kit had taken to using it rather than have its emptiness be a painful reminder to her grandfather of the loss of his wife.

Resting her stocking feet on the footstool shared with the other chair, Kit leaned back to stare at the tongues of flame licking the logs in the fireplace. It and an oil burner provided heat for the small house in the winter. On winter days when the wind was blowing, and there were few days in North Dakota when it didn't, it took both to warm the house. The combination was beginning to thaw Kit now.

She lifted the mug to her lips and sipped at the strong, black coffee, enjoying the reviving heat of the stimulating liquid as it slid down her throat. Her gaze focused on the worn cowboy boots her

grandfather wore, the underslung heels resting on
the footstool near her feet. There were black
marks on the leather made by the constant wearing of spurs. It was more than two years since he'd
been on a horse. Lately he rarely ventured out of
the ranch yard except to go to town.

Sometimes when she looked into his eyes it
seemed she was looking into those of a lost child.
Poor Nate, Kit thought. He had always tried so
hard all of his life, sacrificing his own wants and
needs, and even his pride, to do what he felt was
best for his family. There was compassion in the
glance she lifted to his face, but he was intent on
the letter in his hand.

"Who's that from?" Kit asked, absently curious as she again raised the mug to her lips.

He cleared his throat before answering. "The
new baron." Her classical features hardened into
a steel mask, her fingers whitening in their grip of
the coffee mug. "Do you want to read it?"

"No!" The cup was set aside, the liquid slosh-
ing over the rim to stain the crocheted doily on the
tabletop. Kit pushed herself out of her chair. "We
need another log on the fire," she announced and
walked to the wood box. A long silence followed,
broken only by the sounds of her movement.
When a split log had joined the burning coals of
others amid a shower of sparks, Kit grudgingly
said, "I don't need to read it. You can tell me
what it says."

She remained kneeling in front of the fireplace,

a poker in her hand, jaw clenched. In spite of her wish not to care, Kit had to know what the letter contained.

"It starts out thanking us for our expression of sympathy at the old baron's death and—"

"Sympathy?" Kit blazed, flashing an accusing glance over her shoulder. "You sent a card of condolence?"

Tired brown eyes gazed back at her from a sun-leathered face, asking for her understanding. "I had to make some gesture of acknowledgment of the baron's death. As manager, I sent a card on behalf of the Flying Eagle Ranch for appearance's sake."

Kit turned back to the fire, tears of bitter resentment stinging her eyes. "I hope he rots in hell," she muttered thickly.

"Kitty," Nate Bonner admonished in a low, pain-riddled voice.

She jabbed at the logs with the poker stick, sending more sparks up the chimney. "What else did the new baron have to say?"

She fought the hatred that gnawed at her insides, not wanting to inflict any sense of guilt on her grandfather. As usual, he had meant well.

Sighing, her grandfather hesitated before continuing. "He expresses appreciation for our past loyalty and the hope that it will continue in the future."

"In other words, just keep sending the ranch profits to jolly old England so the new baron can live in the style he's going to become accustomed to.'' The acid-tongued condemnation slipped out, spiteful and bitter. "Damn the man! And damn—''

"Katherine Elisabeth Bonner!" The use of her full given name indicated how thoroughly she had offended his sensibilities. "Martha would turn over in her grave if she heard such words coming from her granddaughter.''

"Yes, grandfather.'' Kit feigned meekness.

Her words brought another sigh and the crackling of paper being folded. "The baron signs off saying that he hopes he will be able to visit the ranch in the near future,'' Nate concluded.

For a moment cold paralysis gripped Kit. "Do you think he will come?''

It was logical for the new baron to want to see his inheritance, to get an idea of the size and amount of his new wealth. On the other hand, he might be content just to receive the monthly reports and monies. She hoped so. She prayed so.

"I guess we'll have to wait and see.'' Nate Bonner slipped the letter back into its envelope and started going through the rest of the mail.

Kit sat back on her heels and stared into the flames. There was not a single part of her body that did not feel the white heat of pride and the burning of injustice.

Absentee ownership of modern ranches in the West was not uncommon, but for the absent owner to be a member of European nobility was.

It hadn't always been that way. During the settling of the American West, vast tracts of land were in the hands of wealthy and often titled Europeans. World wars, depressions and an altering American economy had changed that.

The first Baron Edmonds came to western North Dakota in the 1880s, lured no doubt by the stories of the empire the more illustrious Marquis de Mores was carving in the badlands. The comparison between the French marquis and the English baron ended there. The baron became fascinated by the classless American society. There was no lavish entertainment on the Flying Eagle, no fancy dress balls, no large hunting parties. The young baron worked alongside the men he hired, tried almost to become one of them.

The disastrous winter of 1886 to 1887 struck him as severely as it did other ranchers in the area. Since he had no grandiose schemes such as the Marquis-de Mores had, he didn't quit but rebuilt his cattle herds. When that was done the baron returned to England to visit his ailing mother and came back a year later with a bride, a young woman of rank and breeding, revealing he had not completely conformed to the democratic life-style of the new land.

His new wife did not care for the rigors of frontier life. Within a year there was a baby on the way and the baron returned to England with his wife to await the birth of his heir, promising to come back with his son. He never did set foot again on the Flying Eagle Ranch.

Shortly before the turn of the century, a teenage boy named James Bonner came to work on the ranch for the fall roundup and stayed on for the winter. Ten years later he was still there along with his bride. Three generations of Bonners were born on the ranch, Nate Bonner, his daughter and Kit. Kit loved it fiercely and treated it as her own, with just cause.

Yet, in all these decades, only once had its legal owner seen his property and that had been the grandson of the original baron. Kit had heard his brief visit described many times by her grandparents. That baron was dead. His title and property had been passed on to his male successor. Kit seethed with the unfairness of it.

"What about something to eat?" Her grandfather's voice broke into her thoughts.

Sighing, Kit slowly straightened. "There's some beef stew in the refrigerator. I'll warm it up."

"Why don't you make some biscuits and fix it in the oven the way Martha used to?" Nate suggested.

"All right," she agreed with little enthusiasm.

Although her stomach said she was hungry, Kit wasn't really interested in what she ate. As she walked to the kitchen she saw the first flurry of snowflakes whirling outside the windowpanes. She crossed her fingers that this first blizzard in the month of February would not be as severe as the storm that had ushered out January.

THE WINTER HAD PROVED to be relatively mild and spring had come on time, if a bit blustery. Their calving losses had been at a minimum for a change and the year was off to a good start.

Kit sat astride the blaze-faced bay horse, the shaggy remnants of its winter hair still clinging to its coat. It was a cool May afternoon with a stiff breeze blowing from the north. Her mouth tasted gritty from the fine granules of sand the wind carried. Kit knew it powdered her face.

Her faded brown Stetson was pulled low on her forehead to keep it from being blown off. As always, the golden brown length of her hair was atop her head, tucked in the inside crown of her hat. A long-sleeved, flannel shirt in a green and gold plaid provided warmth from the cool temperature, as did the quilted black vest zipped to the neck. Leather gloves covered the hands holding the reins. Lithe and slim, she resembled a young boy in her faded and patched Levi's and worn-down boots.

Her gaze slowly traveled down the length of fence row. "I swear, Reno," she muttered to the gelding, "I don't see a single break in the fence."

But a half dozen cows and one calf were grazing on the other side of the wire next to the graveled road, proof that somewhere there was a gap in the fence. Dismounting, she looped the reins around a post and took a pair of pliers from the saddlebags.

"First—" she pulled out a staple holding the top strand of barbwire to the post "—we'd better get those cows back in here before they get hit by a car. Then we can look for the hole."

Dropping all three strands and stuffing the staples in her pocket, Kit remounted and walked the snorting bay over the lowered wires. The cows raised their heads as she circled them to drive them back to the home range. One black Angus gave her a wild-eyed look and trotted into the ditch, heading the wrong way.

"You old crow," Kit cursed and reined the bay horse to intercept the cow and turn her back. "I might have known you were leading this bunch. You just can't stay home, can you? Always looking for a loose wire."

With her escape blocked, the Angus rejoined the other cows ambling toward the lowered wires. The cow quickly shouldered her way into the lead and trotted over the lowered wires while the rest followed. They stopped on the other side of the fence, watching as Kit rode the bay over the wires before dismounting to restring them on the post.

Hammering the staple into place again, Kit glanced at the ringleader of the escapees. "I'm not going to keep chasing you back in all summer," she warned. "One more time and you are going to the sale barn."

The other cows drifted away, but the one remained until that section of the fence was again intact and Kit had remounted. There was still the problem of finding where they had got out originally and that meant riding every inch of the fence line. If it wasn't found and repaired, the cow would make use of it again.

It was a boring, tedious job riding fence, but necessary. Kit walked her horse slowly beside the row of posts and barbwire, following the dips and rises of the rugged terrain. Her gaze was alert for any looseness of the wire. Still, she almost rode past the spot. She might never have found it if it hadn't been for a tuft of black hair caught on a barb.

Yet that particular section looked very sturdy. When Kit pushed at the top wire with a gloved hand, she realized its look was deceiving. The wooden fence post had rotted at the base and could be lifted completely off the ground, wire, post and all. Her repairs were flimsy at best. A new steel post was what was needed.

Her ride had taken her nearly to the lane that led from the graveled county road back to the ranch. Kit decided she might as well check out the rest of the fence before heading back. The particular stretch of ground where the lane was relatively level. A flash of sunlight on something metallic caught her eye.

A car was parked half a mile beyond the entrance gate and cattle guard. Kit reined in the bay and stared, at first thinking it might be a neighbor. But the car wasn't one she had seen before. That indicated a stranger, a curiosity seeker or a tourist.

The ranch had always maintained a very low profile, never advertising the identity of its owner. It was a policy that had been in existence long before Kit was born and the privacy of the grounds had been just as jealously guarded since. Whoever the person was, Kit was determined that he or she had better have an excellent reason for trespassing.

Reining the bay in the direction of the car, she touched a spur to its flank to send the horse cantering forward. A man stood near the front of the car, looking off in the opposite direction. At the sound of Kit's approach, he turned and waited.

She stopped the horse a few feet in front of his car and studied the stranger. And he was a stranger. Kit had never seen him before. Tall with a rangy build, he wore a brown corduroy jacket with leather patches at the elbows. The cut of the material seemed to accent the width of his shoulders. A pair of glittering hazel eyes returned her cool look with arrogant ease, and that irritated Kit. The bay horse seemed to sense her sudden flash of tension and stamped restlessly beneath her.

"Were you looking for something?" her husky voice challenged, its tone unfriendly although couched in a polite phrase.

"I'm trying to locate the Flying Eagle Ranch," he informed her in a voice that was low-pitched but with a definite American accent.

Kit's gaze flicked in the direction he had been looking when she had ridden up. "You won't find it out there," she answered shortly.

His mouth thinned into a cold smile at her reply. The movement accented the slashing grooves running from nose to mouth and the lean hollows of his cheeks. The features were harshly masculine from the wide, intelligent forehead, down an aquiline nose to the powerful slant of his jaw. The stiff breeze ruffled the thick dark brown hair growing crisply away from his face.

"I was trying to get a glimpse of the brand on those cattle over there," he explained with a trace of amused contempt. "There wasn't any sign on the gate by the road."

"No, there wasn't," Kit agreed, angered by his attitude. "Are you a salesman?"

"No."

"There isn't any sign on the gate because the Flying Eagle Ranch isn't open to visitors and you are trespassing on private property. About a half a mile up this lane there's a spot where you can turn your car around. Use it."

There was a faint narrowing of his gaze, a gleam entering his eyes that Kit didn't understand. All she knew was that she didn't like it. It made her feel defensive when she was in the right.

"Are you ordering me off?"

Just for an instant something in his tone made Kit question her action. "Are you expected at the ranch?" she countered.

"No, I—"

"Then I'm ordering you to leave," she interrupted briskly and reined the bay to the side of the lane. "And I hope you don't force me to call the county sheriff. Because if I do, you won't get by with a warning. I'll have you arrested."

There were several seconds of charged silence before the man turned and walked to the car door. Kit concealed her surprise. For some reason she simply hadn't expected this man to back down despite her threat. He hadn't seemed the type. He was much too self-assured, or so she had thought.

Now that Kit was no longer transmitting the tenseness of challenge to the bay, the horse stood quietly along the roadside with Kit relaxed in the saddle. A heavy layer of accumulated dust and dirt covered the rear of the car as it drove past her and she wasn't able to see where it was from, but she suspected the license plates were out of state.

There wasn't any reason to wait to see if he obeyed her. Precious working time would be wasted if she waited to see if he used the turn-around a half mile ahead. If he didn't and continued on to the ranch headquarters, Nate or one of the hands would be there to send him on his way.

Turning the horse back toward the fence, Kit listened to the pleasant swishing sound it made as it trotted through the tall, thick grasses. Part of her mind wondered which of the townspeople had let it slip about the ranch. Generally they recognized the ranch's long-held policy of anonymity and respected it. After all, they had the château of a marquis to draw the tourists, and a marquis was certainly better than a baron.

It didn't matter. The stranger would soon be on his way, if not by her order then by someone else's. Kit remembered the prickling of antagonism she had felt when she confronted him, but she had never been easy with strangers, always keeping herself aloof, hardened against them. She had never bemoaned her lack of friends because she had never had any. Hers was a private, solitary existence. That was the best—and safest.

At the fence line she turned and followed it past the closed gate. The brisk wind was quickly blowing away the dust cloud kicked up by the wheels of the car out of sight below the ridge. With a last glance in its direction, Kit dismissed it from her mind and concentrated on the job at hand.

CHAPTER TWO

TIRED AND GRIMY from the long day's work, Kit rode the bay into the ranch yard. Its step was quick, its ears pricked, eager to reach the barn and the night's ration of oats. But Kit noticed Lew Simpson over by the well and turned the reluctant horse away from the barn.

"What's wrong?" She reined the horse to a stop and leaned forward to see for herself.

Lew Simpson was on the other side of forty, a short, wiry man. The sweat-stained hat he wore concealed the fact that he had only half a halo of hair, the top of his head virtually bald. He'd come to work for the Flying Eagle before Kit was born and had been a mentor, an uncle and a workmate. In a typical cowboy fashion he worked hard and played harder.

"The pump was actin' up." He wiped the grease from his hands onto his Levi's and reached for the cover that protected the motor. "I guess it needed a little oil and some cussin'. It's runnin' fine now."

"Good." Kit sat back in the saddle.

"Did ya—"

The clink of metal against metal diverted her attention to the shed. The tractor was parked in front of it and Kit could see someone kneeling next to the front wheels.

"What's wrong with the H?" she demanded.

"I think Kyle's busted it again," Lew answered.

Kit drew in a quick angry breath and held it for a second before snapping an order. "About a quarter mile west of the gate a fence post has rotted through at the base. Tomorrow I want you to take one of the new steel posts from the shed out there and replace it. I temporarily jerry-rigged it, but it will never hold."

Without waiting for an acknowledgment she spurred the bay around and hurried him to the shed. Her expression had hardened into forbiddingly grim lines when she stopped a few feet from the crouching figure.

"What happened?" Her husky voice was harsh and cutting.

The man didn't look up, but Kit saw the dull flush creep into his freckled face. Kyle Johanson was no older than Kit, a town boy who had decided ranching was going to be his profession. He'd barely known one end of the horse from the other when he had signed on over a year ago, but he tried hard, too hard sometimes, and was ridiculously careless other times. His saving grace was that he was very mechanically minded, but he seemed to break things just to repair them.

"It's the steering rod, I think." He shifted

uneasily and pretended to peer at the wheels in a study of concentration. "It might be busted."

"How did it happen?" Kit demanded.

"I hit a rut. That last rain really tore up the road," he hedged. "I was headed for the yard when Frank came and told me—"

"Hot-dogging it again, I suppose," she lashed out, impatient with his endless variety of excuses. "When are you going to learn that tractors aren't made for racing? You can't go galloping around on them like a horse!"

"I know," he murmured lamely.

"I want that tractor fixed by tomorrow," Kit snapped. "And I don't give a damn whether you have to drive to Bismarck or Billings to find the parts. You got that?"

"Yes, ma'am," he mumbled, but his light blue eyes flashed her a look of rebellious anger despite his subservient response.

Kit knew the reason. However justified the tongue-lashing might be, his manly pride resented that it came from a female. She checked her temper and nudged the horse away from the tractor, aware that if he voiced any objection to her authority she would have to fire him. Just now, she couldn't afford to spend the time looking for more help. Discretion insisted that she retreat and not push him any further.

As Kit walked the horse away she heard Kyle mutter, "What's got into her anyway? She had no call to crawl on me like that. I didn't do it on purpose."

Lew must have been approaching as she left, because she heard him answer, in a consoling and faintly guarded tone, "Everybody has a bad day now and again, boy."

"She's a regular shrew. It's no wonder nobody ever asks her out. She acts like a damned virgin queen inst—"

"That's enough, boy." Lew's voice sliced off the rest of the sentence.

There was a brief stab of pain in her chest, but Kit lifted her chin and rode a little straighter in the saddle.

Bitterly, she wondered who it was that had said words were not sticks and stones. She had learned long ago that it was a lie.

Her diagonal route across the ranch yard to the barn took Kit directly past the front porch of the Big House with its stout log columns. The rough-cut planking of its exterior walls resembled pictures she had seen of hunting lodges in the Rockies. The sprawling, one-story structure was impressive in its rustic simplicity, blending with the rugged splendor of the Dakota badlands.

Usually Kit avoided even glancing at the Big House, but her eyes were drawn to it by some inner compulsion. The lowering sun cast a long patch of light into the shadows of the porch and she could see the heavy wooden front door standing open. Vaguely she remembered Nate saying something about airing the house this morning and she supposed that he had neglected to shut it up. He seemed to be becoming more and more absentminded about some things.

Impatiently she turned the bay gelding toward the hitching rail in front of the porch. Dismounting, Kit wrapped the reins loosely around the rail and walked up the three steps to the porch, her spurs jingling faintly.

The sound of her footsteps echoed hollowly on the planked floorboards as she walked across the porch to the screen door. Reaching to close the front door, Kit hesitated. Nate had probably opened windows in the house, she decided, and reached to open the screen door instead.

Entering the wide entrance hall, Kit paused, fighting the waves of bitter and hostile resentment the house always caused to well within her. The cool breeze filtering through the rooms had not banished all the staleness from the air and its musty odor filled her nose.

A half a dozen steps into the hallway, Kit noticed the door to the library-den standing open. Her nerves tensed, their ends suddenly raw and exposed. Unwillingly she let her gaze be pulled to the open door and into the room.

The blackened hearth of a fireplace made of red brick was on the outer wall directly opposite the door. On the floor in front of it was the brown hide of a grizzly bear, its yellow white fanglike teeth bared in a permanent snarl. It was a trophy of the first baron, hunted and killed when it began marauding the ranch's cattle herds. The grizzly had probably been one of the last in the badlands, the predatory species now extinct in the area like the wolf and the cougar.

But it wasn't the bearskin rug that captured Kit's attention. It was the portrait above the fireplace mantel. Despite the dimness of the room, illuminated only by the sunlight glimmering through the dusty windowpanes, Kit could still make out the features of the face in oils.

Against a background of light blue was the face of a man in his prime. Waving, sand-colored hair fell across his smooth forehead at a rakish angle. Despite the somber lines of his handsome features, there was a wickedly engaging glint to the blue eyes staring back at Kit and drawing her into the room with the irresistible pull of metal to a magnet.

Her fingers slowly curled into her palms, turning her hands into tight, gloved fists. A seemingly bottomless hatred glittered savagely in her brown eyes as she gazed at the image of the grandson of the first baron. The violence of her raging emotions trembled through her, stiffening every sinew into finely tempered steel. Not even the knowledge that he was dead lessened her reaction to his portrait.

Searing anger and resentment coursed through her veins. It seethed like a volcano on the verge of eruption, white-hot heat firing her blood. It was a

fury that refused to be subdued or suppressed, revealed in every taut line of her vibrating body and
the clenched fists held rigidly at her side. Scalding
tears sprang into her eyes, Kit's only means of
emotional release, but not one slipped over the
dam of her lashes.

"Was there something you wanted?"

The blandly arrogant voice of a stranger
shocked Kit out of her trance. She pivoted in its
direction, her eyes rounded and momentarily
alarmed. Her total concentration with the portrait
had blinded her to the figure sitting behind the
hardwood desk. It was the stranger from the road,
the one she had ordered off the property. His
relaxed air, his attitude of being completely in
possession and command, was the igniting spark
to her temper.

In the blink of an eye, surprise was overtaken by
the violence that had a moment ago been directed
impotently at the portrait. Now there was someone it could be released on, and justly, too.

"I warned you to get off this ranch!" Kit
unleashed the fury that had been boiling within
her. "What are you doing here? Who let you in?"
She'd have their scalp and his, too, before she was
done.

Her demand briefly arched a dark brow, but
nothing resembling guilt or any other emotion
flickered in the cool hazel eyes regarding her so
steadily. The rough angles and planes of his face
were immobile.

"No one *let* me in." He stressed the verb. The cruel line of his lips parted as he spoke, baring white teeth in a cynically cold smile that mocked her wrath.

His insolence was an electric prod and Kit stormed toward the hallway. "Someone is sure as hell going to show you out!"

Not even in the blazing red of her anger was Kit so foolish as to believe she could throw him out. And she sincerely hoped the stranger would not go peaceably because she would love to see him roughed up a bit and that complacent look literally wiped from his face.

Her angry strides were punctuated by the sharp jingle of her spurs. As she neared the door she could see Lew and Kyle walking by through the fine mesh of the screen. Her outstretched arm violently pushed the door open, rigidly holding it ajar.

"Lew! Kyle!" Her gravelly voice barked their names.

Both heads jerked around toward the Big House, their steps halting at the strident tone of her voice. There was a faintly puzzled look to their expressions, visible at even Kit's distance.

"Come here!" she ordered. "There's a gentleman—"

"We already met the new baron, Kit," Lew interposed, frowning and cocking his head to the side. "So if it ain't too important, Kyle and me got to make some phone calls to see if we can find the replacement parts for the H."

The last part of his reply didn't register, only the first—only the words "the new baron." Every tissue froze. There was a wild hammering in her head. It took Kit a second to realize it was the sound of her own heartbeat pounding in her ears like a thousand war drums.

In slow motion she let the screen door swing shut and saw the two ranch hands hesitate before walking on. With equally deliberate movements Kit turned.

The stranger—savagely she corrected it—the new baron was negligently leaning a shoulder against the jamb of the opened library door. The side of his forefinger was thoughtfully rubbing across the line of his mouth, his veiled but watchful look studying her reaction.

"You are the new baron." The bitter words were an accusation, issued precisely without any attempt to disguise her dislike of the news.

He straightened to his full height, the hand falling easily away from his mouth. Yet there still remained something indolent about his pose. A faint, almost imperceptible nod of his head acknowledged the truth of her accusation.

"The name is Reese Talbot," he offered in further identification, without in any way being ingratiating or friendly. It was a flat statement.

"Why didn't you tell me who you were?" Kit demanded in a low, boiling voice, incensed that he had deliberately kept her in the dark when she had confronted him on the lane.

He tipped his head slightly sideways, his gaze hardening. "I'm not in the habit of explaining myself to fuzz-faced punks."

She was trembling with the force of her contained anger. "What am I supposed to do now? Should I curtsy and beg m'lord's forgiveness for not knowing who he was?"

His eyes narrowed into gold brown slits, his gaze slowly raking her from head to toe. Kit became conscious of her appearance. Her stained hat was pulled low on her head, concealing the hair piled beneath it. A powdering of dust covered her face. She could taste the caked grime on her lips. The man's shirt, the patched Levi's and the bulky quilted vest combined to make her figure shapelessly slender. Spurs were strapped on her boots and leather gloves covered her hands.

A light glittered in his eyes, amused contempt. "You could never guess by looking at you that you are a woman. But then, I didn't expect to meet a man-talking female, either."

"If you think I'm going to object to being mistaken for a boy, you are wrong," Kit retorted.

But he didn't indicate one way or the other what he thought. "You obviously work here."

Kit hesitated for a fraction of a second. Evidently the new baron, this Reese Talbot, didn't know who she was. In a way it was hardly surprising.

"Yes, I work here," she admitted and added no more.

He continued to regard her in that same light. "What's your name?"

"Katheri—" For some reason she almost gave him her full given name, as if asserting her femininity, but she quickly changed it. "Kit Bonner."

"Bonner," he repeated the last name. "That's the same as the ranch manager. Are you his granddaughter?"

"Yes." Kit tensed, suddenly defensive, her chin lifting. "How did you know?"

"He mentioned you when I met him this afternoon." Reese Talbot seemed to find her question curious. It showed in the sharpening of his look. "He said you'd ridden off somewhere."

"And you presumed that meant a leisurely afternoon horseback ride," she added contemptuously. "An idle canter through the meadow."

"Yes, I did."

Kit had difficulty holding his level gaze and looked away in irritation. "Why have you come here?" Her demanding question short and challenging.

"I own the Flying Eagle. I wasn't aware I required a reason to come here," he said in a voice that was as smooth as steel.

Its thrusting gibe found a sensitive spot. "You aren't wanted." Kit was struggling so hard to keep control of her anger that her voice was even huskier than usual.

"Obviously not by you." Reese Talbot seemed to find her open hostility a source of amusement.

"Not by anyone," she corrected stiffly. "Any welcome you've received since you arrived was only issued out of polite courtesy."

"And you don't feel you are bound by any rules of courtesy." He was taunting her as one would tease a hissing kitten.

Kit trembled from the frustration of her own impotence. "I am not a hypocrite. And I am not about to mouth polite phrases I don't mean."

"That would be asking too much, wouldn't it?" he said mockingly.

"It isn't so strange that I'm skeptical of your reason for coming since you descended on us without warning."

There was an indication of thinning patience in the hardening set of his jaw. The slight crook to his nose gave a forbidding air to his lean, classically and aggressively male features.

"Perhaps I merely wanted to insure that my arrival would be minus a lot of fanfare," he suggested.

"And perhaps you thought your new inheritance wasn't sending you enough money!" Kit flashed. "Perhaps you thought if you arrived unannounced, it would be easier to discover if we were stealing from you. As you can see—" her hand slashed through the air in a sweeping gesture to encompass an invisible everything "—we are all living high off the hog. We just keep replacing worn-out equipment parts and keep track of every stray cow or calf for the fun of it."

"For your grandfather's sake, I think it would be best if you didn't say any more, Miss Bonner." There was no mistaking the unspoken threat behind his words.

Kit paled that he should dare to threaten her, but she swallowed the bitter words that rose like bile in her throat and turned to leave, wanting to get as far away from him as possible, his presence becoming a suffocating thing.

"Don't leave yet, Miss Bonner. I'm not through with you."

His mocking and autocratic voice flashed through her like a lightning bolt, searing her limbs and jerking Kit up short. Fighting for every ounce of composure she possessed, Kit faced him, her brown eyes snapping.

"Do I require your permission to leave?" she blazed.

He ignored her rebellious stance. "Your grandfather suggested that I speak to you about the house."

Her indignant anger was tempered by caution at the sound of the two magic words, grandfather and house. "What house?" Kit demanded guardedly, lowering her head so the wide brim of her Stetson shadowed most of her expression.

"This house, of course." His reply was smooth enough, but a frown flickered across Reese Talbot's forehead.

"What about it?"

"It needs more than just an airing. It needs a

thorough cleaning and the cupboards need to be stocked with food.''

"The fact that it isn't ready for you is your own fault since you didn't notify us that you were coming," she stated.

"I am aware of the reason, but that doesn't change the situation, does it?" Again there was that flash of white teeth in a cold smile.

"How long are you intending to stay?"

"I have no idea," he responded in a tone that indicated it had no bearing on the matter.

"I am neither a housekeeper nor a cook." Her chin was thrust forward at a defiant angle. "So however long your visit turns out to be, you are going to have to find your own solution."

"And in the interim?" he challenged.

"As for bedding, I imagine the boys could rustle you up some clean blankets and such from the bunkhouse. And for your evening meal—" if he thought she was going to invite him to join her and Nate he was mistaken again "—Cookie—Frank Jarvis does all the cooking for the boys. I'm sure he can stretch the meal to include you."

With an abrupt pivot Kit was out of the house, letting the screen door slam behind her. She half expected to hear him order her back into the house as she clumped down the steps to the hitching post where the bay horse waited patiently. Not a single sound came from the house.

Looping the reins over the horse's neck she swung into the saddle and jabbed a spur into the horse's flank, sending him bounding forward toward the barn. There she dismounted, stripped the saddle and pad from his back and led him into the corral where she unbuckled the bridle. All her actions were accomplished with the swiftness of controlled anger.

As she stowed the saddle and bridle in the tack room, Frank was graining the horses they kept at the ranch yard. Kit ignored his greeting. Like Lew, Frank had been around for a while and wisely didn't pursue a response. With the riding gear put away, Kit left the barn and headed straight for the small house, keeping her gaze averted from the Big House.

The hinges of the door squeaked as she pulled it open. The sound immediately brought an anxious call from her grandfather. "Kitty, is that you?"

"Yes." He was closer, in the kitchen now.

"If you are going to tell me that the baron has arrived, I already know it." Unzipping the vest, Kit shrugged out of it and hung it on a coat hook. Then the spurs came off, followed by the hat.

"Have you talked to him yet?" Nate Bonner asked finally and quietly, already guessing the answer by the abruptness of her movement.

"Yes, I've talked to him." She brushed past him into the kitchen.

"Kitty, you can't blame him for what happened." Her grandfather followed, anxious yet gently understanding. "He had nothing to do with it."

"I don't blame him for it. All of that happened so long ago that it really isn't important anymore," she lied through her teeth. It had molded her life, erected the hard shell around her that never let anyone through. Kit stopped beside the counter and glanced at the condensing steam on the glass cover of the crockpot. "It looks like dinner will hold for half an hour. I'm going to take a shower and change into some clean clothes before we eat."

Further discussion of the baron's arrival was avoided. The subject was not mentioned once during the evening meal. Kit rose from the small table in the kitchen to carry the dishes to the sink.

Nate cleared his throat and announced, "The new baron has invited us over to the Big House tonight."

"You go," she replied calmly and without hesitation. "I have a lot of paperwork to do."

"The invitation was for both of us."

"But it was made before the baron knew who your granddaughter was. Now that he's met me, I don't think he'll be at all sorry if I don't accept." The plates were in the sink and she reached for the milk glasses.

"What happened this afternoon when you met him?" He held a match to his pipe and puffed.

"I thought he was trespassing, a tourist or a newspaper reporter or something, and I ordered him off the ranch. He attempted to put me in my place."

Her clipped answer drew a long sigh from Nate Bonner. "I don't think he knows anything about you or what happened. He seemed surprised that I had a granddaughter. Maybe it would be best if I explained—"

"Don't you dare!" The facade of composure shattered as Kit pivoted to face him. The resentment smoldering within surfaced to blaze in her eyes. Quickly she tried to stamp out the fires. "It wouldn't change anything." Kit turned back to the sink. "So if he doesn't know, it wouldn't do any good to enlighten him. Besides, I doubt if he'll be here very long. None of the barons ever do stay. They just grace the ranch with their presence for a short while," she offered bitterly, "then go back to their castles in England."

"You're probably right," Nate agreed, biting the stem of his pipe as he spoke, a faint grimness to his words.

"Of course I'm right. That's their pattern. So why should this baron behave any differently than the others?" She shrugged. "He'll go and everything will be the way it was before he came."

"Not always," Nate murmured to himself as he pushed out of the kitchen chair. "Not always."

Her heart stopped beating for a second, an icy chill running down her spine. She clamped her teeth together, gritting them in a self-willing determination that it would turn out the way she said. His presence would cause no more than a mere ripple from a pebble in a large pond, and not the reverberating splash of a boulder.

"I'll be going to the Big House now," Nate announced.

"All right. As soon as I'm done with the dishes, I'm going to get at the paperwork."

"I probably won't be long."

"No, I don't imagine," she agreed. Standing at the sink, her hand poised on the faucet knob, Kit heard herself whisper, "Don't tell him, grandpa."

His hand rested briefly on her shoulder, a fleeting caress of understanding and reassurance. "I won't, child."

She turned on the faucet, pride stiffening her carriage and instilling a note of cynical indifference into her voice. "Give the baron my regards."

As the back door closed behind her grandfather, Kit felt her protective veneer crumbling, a harsh, splintering sound within her. No matter how much she tried to deny it, she was vulnerable, frighteningly so. That's why she had to act so tough, so insensitive.

CHAPTER THREE

By MORNING the defensive shell was again in place, erected even sturdier than before. The ranch's lone milk cow, kept to supply their needs, had been milked and her morning offering was now strained and in the refrigerator.

Dressed in her usual garb of hat, man's shirt, worn Levi's and boots, Kit was returning to the barn. The sight of Lew wearing his going-to-town outfit of a good print shirt and crisp denims, heading for the ranch pickup, changed her direction.

"Where are you going, Lew?" she demanded. "I thought I told you to put that new fence post in this morning."

"You did, but the baron asked me to take him into town." He gestured toward the Big House in explanation.

A film of red sprang before her eyes. "I don't give a damn what the baron wants!" Kit flamed. "You'll do as you're told."

"Don't you go gettin' on your high horse with me, Kitty Bonner," Lew stiffened. "Don't you forget I knowed you when you was waddlin' around this place in diapers."

"And don't you forget that I'm the boss," she retorted. "I give the orders around here."

"I was under the impression," a low voice said behind Kit, whirling her around like a top, "that as the owner I had something to say about what goes on here."

Reese Talbot confronted her, complacent challenge in his cold smile and hooded eyes. Kit hadn't heard him approach and to find him standing so close caught her by surprise. At close quarters his height was intimidating, as was the breadth of his shoulders. Disturbingly vital so early in the morning, he seemed an immovable male object planted squarely in her path. Attacking a superior force was useless, which made defense mandatory.

"Of course you have a say in what goes on." The reluctant admission was issued in a clipped tone. "But it's wiser not to go around countermanding orders until you know what's going on. The fence along the road needs repairing. And I can't have one of my men wasting valuable time standing around a saloon drinking beer while waiting on your pleasure to return to the ranch."

"One of *your* men, Miss Bonner?" His tauntingly soft voice put emphasis on the possessive pronoun.

The grounds for her answer were too shaky so Kit sidestepped the question by flicking a sharp glance at the ranch hand listening in. "Get into some work clothes, Lew, and get out on that fence line." Then her challenging gaze reverted to

Reese Talbot. "What's the matter with your car?"

"It acquired a flat tire overnight and the spare is in the same deflated state." Reese Talbot offered this explanation with his dark head drawn back, a glimmer of superior amusement in his expression. "When I mentioned it to Lew, he was going in to town with the pickup and suggested I ride along."

The answer drew Kit's attention to the ranch hand. "And why were you going in to town?" she demanded.

Lew shifted, revealing unease. "Sorrell junked one of his tractors and has been sellin' the parts. I thought I'd check to see if the steerin' column could be interchanged or modified to fit the H. His place is only a mile or so from town so I figured that was no sense in makin' two trips in the same direction."

"You figured," Kit repeated in an angry under-breath. "And what about the fence?"

"I was going to do it this afternoon."

"After you blew a whole morning in town?"

"I think you'd better go fix the fence, Lew," Reese Talbot suggested dryly. "Miss Bonner can take me to town and check on that tractor part for you."

"Yessir." Lew bobbed his head in agreement and moved away, obeying this order when he had more or less ignored Kit's.

That irritated, as did that indefinable air of authority that emanated from the man before her. The fact that he had commandeered her services as chauffeur did not set well, either. Kit was about to inform him that as well as not being a cook and a housekeeper, she was also not a chauffeur, but she didn't have the chance.

"I was under the impression, Miss Bonner—" there was nothing amused about the narrowed look he gave her "—that your grandfather was the manager of this ranch and as such was the one to give the orders, not you."

The ground seemed to rock beneath her feet. It was one thing for her to know that Nate had lost interest in the ranch since his wife's death and had begun neglecting his duties, and another thing for Reese Talbot to know. A sense of loyalty made Kit protect her grandfather from discovery.

"He is," she defended. "I take my orders from him."

"I see," he murmured, but Kit saw that his suspicion hadn't been completely set aside. "Is there anything specific you are to do this morning or are you free to drive to town?"

Her decision was made in a flash. "I can drive you to town."

"Good." Reese glanced at the gold of his watch, glistening around his tanned wrist. "Is ten minutes long enough for you to change?"

"There's nothing wrong with the way I'm dressed," she countered smoothly. It was part of her armor, a protective shield that kept her aloof from others, and that was what Kit wanted. "Why should I change?"

There was a quirking lift to one corner of his mouth as he ran a mocking eye over her decidedly masculine attire that gave her a shapeless form. "Why, indeed?"

"If you are ready to leave, I am," Kit challenged.

An upturned palm gestured toward the pickup truck parked a few feet away, indicating his readiness. Kit walked to the driver's side, aware that he followed. She felt her nerves tautening as she realized that she had sentenced herself to spending the better part of the morning in his company. It wasn't wise, not when her emotions ran so high against him. Or at least against the injustice his presence represented.

By the time Reese Talbot had climbed into the other side of the cab, Kit had started the motor and was shifting the truck into gear. They bounced out of the rough ranch yard onto the equally jolting ruts of the lane, springs squeaking in protest as they tried to absorb the shock of the bumpy ride. Kit knew if she slowed down it wouldn't be so rough, but, perversely, she didn't.

"Why hasn't the road been regraded?" Reese questioned, riding out the jolts with apparent ease.

"There's no point in it—not until summer." Kit kept a firm hold on the steering wheel to prevent it being wrenched from her hands. "We don't get much rain here, but when we do get a spring rainstorm it's usually a violent one." Her response was matter-of-fact. "So the downpour washes out the roadbed."

The jarring ride continued until they reached the relative smoothness of the scorialike gravel of the county road, which left a haze of red dust behind them. Kit's attention was divided between the road, twisting, climbing and dipping as it snaked its way through the torturous landscape, and the scenic badlands themselves.

Its wild terrain was one that Kit never tired of seeing. Stark buttes jutted into the horizon. The layered rock faces of bluffs offered a striation of color from the bricklike red of baked clay to yellow and buff with an occasional stripe of black, a seam of low-grade lignite coal.

Dominating it all was the tall, thick grass, green and rich, the priceless bounty of the so-called badlands. Its dense cover was interspersed with sagebrush and wild flowers. In the twisting ravines formed by runoffs and along the winding streambeds, the cottonwoods and willow trees flourished, while stands of junipers clung to the north slopes.

At times it seemed a maze of canyons and gullies and mesas, verdant pastures and impassable rock cliffs. But always it stunned the eyes, awed the viewer, and the wild pulse beat of an untameable land became Kit's own.

"How old are you?"

The question banished her absorption and Kit became aware of the man seated in the pickup cab beside her. That unrevealing gaze of his was watching her and probably had been for some time. The penetrating scrutiny prickled her nerve ends.

"Twenty-one. How old are you?" She returned the challenge with piercing calm.

"Thirty-five."

"You look older." Kit kept her gaze fixed on the road as they topped a rise.

"Who put the chip on your shoulder?"

"I don't know what you mean," she murmured coolly.

"Come now, Miss Bonner," he taunted her skeptically. Without looking at him Kit could still see the faint curl of his lip in a cynical smile. "Ever since our first meeting you've been trying to impress upon me how hard and tough you are."

"I don't know what you are talking about." But Kit felt her muscles tensing, although she continued to avoid looking in his direction.

"I am impressed," he offered, but not without some amusement. "You have the hardest shell I've ever seen."

"What makes you think it's only a shell?"

"Because, as much as you might not like to admit it, you are still made of flesh and blood like the rest of us."

There was the rasping sound of flint being struck and Kit glanced over to see the first wisp of smoke curling from the tip of the cigarette between his lips. The aromatic scent of tobacco smoke was inviting, its implied taste promising a narcotic balm for her nerves.

"May I have a cigarette?" Kit requested.

"They are...tailor-made." The glint in his gold brown eyes appeared to be laughing at her.

"So?" she frowned.

Reese took another cigarette from the pack and lighted it. "I assumed that you either chewed tobacco or rolled your own cigarettes." He handed the second one to her. "I've heard rolling your own is considered a 'manly' art."

Kit gritted her teeth at his gibe, knowing he was taunting her lack of feminine mannerisms. She inhaled on the filtered end of the cigarette, the taste of his mouth still warm on the paper. It wasn't a sensation she cared for.

"I'll have to try it sometime, won't I?" was her bland response to his comment.

If anyone had ever got used to teasing, malicious or otherwise, Kit had. Her aloofness, her coolness, had deflected many a previous comment. And it didn't desert her now. It had been years since anyone had been able to tell if his remark had found its target.

"What happened to your parents?" Reese switched subjects without appearing to care that he hadn't aroused a more heated reaction.

"They're dead. Nate and Martha raised me." As an afterthought she added the explanation, "My grandparents."

"You're doing it again," he observed.

"Doing what?" Kit darted him another frowning glance.

"You're trying to prove how tough and independent you are by using your grandparents' given names. Calling them granddad and grandma would imply a closeness, a dependency, and you seem determined not to need anybody." His speculating glance made itself felt even though Kit kept her gaze focused on the road. "What did you call your parents?"

"I don't remember. I doubt if I ever got past 'mama' and 'dada,'" she said, lifting her shoulders in a characteristic and silently defensive shrug. "I don't remember either of them. They are just names of people I've seen in photographs."

"And do you regret that?"

As far as Kit was concerned, this delving had gone far enough. "What is this, baron? A psychoanalysis?"

"The name is Reese. If you have difficulty getting that out I'll settle for Talbot, but no title, please." It was more of an order than a mere statement.

"Why not?" Kit challenged. "You inherited the title along with everything else, didn't you?"

"I have no use for the title." Reese Talbot ground his cigarette out in the truck's ashtray. "I'm a U.S. citizen, not a British subject."

"Surely it will come in handy in England, though, when you spend a few days at your castle?'' There was the acid of bitter sarcasm flowing through the murmured question.

"I'm sorry to disappoint you, but there is no castle in England, not anymore."

"Oh? Did you sell it?"

"Not me. My predecessor disposed of it some years ago."

"What a pity for you," Kit offered. "A title with no castle."

"It was too costly to maintain. If he hadn't sold it, I would have."

Kit gave him a long look, studying his profile, aquiline and noble. "I understood you inherited a fortune."

Her gaze fell away when his swung to meet it, arrogant and mocking. "Are you probing into your employer's private affairs, Katherine?" The way his low voice rolled so tauntingly over her given name vibrated over her skin, pricking the hairs at the back of her neck. But Reese Talbot didn't wait for a response. "Actually after the death duties—the inheritance taxes—there was very little left."

"Except the Flying Eagle, isn't that right, baron?" she gibed, jealousy surfacing for an emerald second.

"Yes, except for the Flying Eagle, baroness."

Her stomach lurched at the feminine title. "Why did you call me that?" Kit demanded, flashing him an angry glance.

"You didn't like it?"

"No, I didn't like it!" she snapped.

"Neither do I. So let's drop the 'baron.' "

His clipped order coincided with their arrival in town. Kit didn't acknowledge the order, instead she pointed out the red roof of the château built as a summer home by the ambitious Marquis de Mores in the early 1880s. It was visible through the budding trees, located on a hill overlooking the town of Medora, named for his American wife, and the perpetually carving waters of the Little Missouri River, responsible for creating the North Dakota badlands.

Their first stop was at a service station to leave the flat tire to be repaired. Kit was fully conscious of the questioning and curious looks she received. The few times she was ever seen in the company of a man it had always been someone from the ranch, mainly Lew or Frank or her grandfather. It was obvious to even the most casual observer that Reese Talbot was not your average cowhand, if he could be mistaken for a cowboy at all. But since he didn't see fit to identify himself, neither did Kit.

"Where to now?" Kit let the truck idle in the station's driveway.

"I want to see if I can arrange to hire someone locally to do the cooking and the housecleaning for me."

"I'll leave you in town then," she stated, slipping the truck into gear and easing her foot down on the accelerator.

"Where are you going? To see about the tractor part?" he questioned.

"Yes." She turned onto the main street, its rustic old buildings restored. "I wouldn't worry about finding someone. You'll have a flood of applicants for the job," Kit offered cynically, "especially when people find out who you are."

"Is there anyone you would care to recommend?"

"No one. You are on your own, bar—Mr. Talbot," she corrected and pulled the truck close to the curb to let him out.

"What time shall I meet you?" Reese stepped out of the cab of the truck and leaned against the open window frame to look back at her.

"Medora isn't all that big," Kit stated. "When I'm finished, I'll find you."

The glinting light in his eye seemed to laugh at her attempted assertion of superiority. Despite his amusement, Kit had a warm sense of satisfaction as she drove away to complete her own errands.

But it was nearly noon before she got back into town. There had been one frustrating obstacle on top of another, first in finding Sorrell and then in trying to determine whether his part would fit the damaged one in the ranch's tractor.

It was nearing the Memorial Day week, which meant there was a scattering of tourists in town. Kit looked at many faces as she drove down the street, without seeing Reese. Finally she parked the pickup in front of the post office and continued the search on foot.

Ignoring the curious looks from the tourists as
they wondered if they were seeing a real live cowboy—or was it a cowgirl—Kit walked down the
street, her head turning and looking, peering into
storefronts for a glimpse of the man she sought.
The main area of Medora covered no more than a
few blocks and Kit walked it all.

She turned and began to retrace her route to the
pickup. As she passed by the Rough Rider Hotel,
Kit was about to decide that Reese had given up
waiting for her and had found some other means
of transportation back to the ranch.

The side entrance door to the hotel, leading to
the restaurant, opened. "Are you looking for
me?" Reese stood in the door frame, seeming to
fill it.

Kit stopped abruptly. "Yes, and it appears that
I found you." She wasn't about to admit that she
had any trouble.

"I got tired of cooling my heels waiting for you
and decided to have some lunch. Join me?" He
stepped backward into the hotel, an outstretched
arm holding the door open for Kit, leaving her little option but to agree.

Before she was two steps into the hall a set of
strong fingers clamped on her elbow and the
strength of his grip momentarily surprised Kit.
Reese Talbot had struck her as being in good physical shape, but the degree of his fitness was dis-
concerting. Her upturned glance met the veiled
glitter of his look and Kit felt a surge of resentment at the way he always seemed to be laughing

at her, although there wasn't a ghost of a smile on that hard mouth.

"My table is this way," he explained and directed her to the room on the right.

Their destination was a table for two set against the far wall away from the mainstream of traffic. Kit was glad of its location. It made her feel protected, free from curious and prying eyes. Coffee and a water glass were on the table in front of one chair and Kit walked to the opposite side, pulling out the chair and sitting down before Reese could courteously offer assistance.

"Aren't you going to take off your hat?" his low voice mocked her. His hand was on the back of her chair as Kit drew it up to the table.

"No."

"With any other woman, I would suspect that her hair was a mess and vanity refused to let her be seen in public looking less than her best." Reese walked to his chair to sit opposite her, running his gaze over her face. "With you I suspect it's a case of stubbornness and nonconformity.

"You could be right," was all Kit would admit.

The grooves deepened around his mouth, the only hint of a smile he displayed at her response. "I haven't been served yet. Would you like to order something?"

"I think I'll have a sandwich," she agreed practically. She was hungry and Nate would have fixed his own lunch by now. Eating here would save having to scrape together a hurried meal when they returned to the ranch.

Reese motioned to the waitress, who brought over a menu. Kit glanced briefly at the sandwich selection and gave her order to the young girl. Not wanting to engage in any more small talk with Reese, she began studying the western paintings on the walls, a complementing touch to the rustic motif of the dining room. Among the paintings were photographs of Teddy Roosevelt, the twenty-sixth president of the United States, and a former rancher in the badlands at approximately the same time as the Marquis de Mores and the first baron who started the Flying Eagle.

"Kit?" A questioning female voice broke into her concentration. "Kit Bonner? It is you, isn't it?"

She glanced around to see a blond-haired woman about her age approaching the table hesitantly. A defensively proud mask stole over Kit's smooth features as she recognized a former classmate at school.

When the blonde got a full view of Kit's face she broke into a smile. "It is you, Kit," she declared in delight. "I was sitting over at that table when you came in and I said to my girl friend, 'That looks like Kit Bonner. I used to go to school with her.' But I wasn't sure it was you."

"Hello, Carolyn." Kit offered the greeting stiffly, wary of the woman's motives for seeking her out.

"My gosh, it's been ages since I've seen you."
The declaration was accompanied by a short,
amazed laugh. "Not since we graduated, right?"

"I think so," she nodded.

Kit remembered her more clearly now, and the
overtures of friendship Carolyn Nesbitt had made
in those school years. But Kit had been leery, just
as she had been leery of all attempts by others to
get into her confidence. Yet Carolyn seemed genu-
inely glad to see her again after all this time. It was
a very warming sensation and her lips softened into a wary smile.

"How have you been? You look wonderful,
Kit." Blue eyes sparkled over the golden tan of
Kit's complexion.

"I'm fine. And you?" she returned.

"Great. I'm married now, you know." Her left
hand was lifted to show off the wedding rings.
"It's Carolyn Quinlan now. No little ones yet,
though. Bob and I are waiting for a couple of
years before starting a family."

"I wish you both the best of luck," Kit offered
and suddenly became aware of Reese standing patiently and courteously beside the table.

At some point in their initial greeting, he must
have risen while all her attention had been focused
on Carolyn. The gold flecks in his hazel eyes glittered alertly, his gaze directed solely at her. The
expression on his bluntly sculpted features was
unreadable, but Kit was aware that she had been
under microscopic study for the last several

minutes. It was disquieting to discover he had
been observing her all this time and she felt herself
bristling at his invasion of her privacy.

When she glanced back to Carolyn, she realized
she had drawn the blonde's attention to Reese.
Since he persisted in standing there with such formal courtesy, it was impossible to ignore him. Kit
could see the curiosity forming in Carolyn's face
and his action had made it imperative that she in-
troduce them.

"This is Carolyn. . .Quinlan. We went to school
together," she said to Reese, informing him of
facts he had probably already acquired from their
conversation.

"So I gathered," he said with an undertone of
mockery, his gaze now fixed on the blond woman
facing him.

"Carolyn, this is—" Kit hesitated a fraction of
a second before announcing in a husky but challenging voice "—the owner of the Flying Eagle,
the new baron." She stressed his title and received
a sharp look of censure from Reese.

The blonde was plainly flustered by his identity,
her color fluctuating wildly. Incapable of speech,
Carolyn seemed to be trying to make up her mind
whether she should curtsy or merely bob her head
in humble acknowledgment. Embarrassed and
awed, she couldn't do either. Kit felt sorry for her,
but she hadn't guessed that her former classmate
would be so overwhelmed.

Reese took charge of the situation, extending a

hand and flashing her a smile filled with potent male charm. "The name is Reese Talbot, Mrs. Quinłan." Deliberately he didn't notice how awkwardly Carolyn shook his hand.

"How do you do, sir," Carolyn mumbled.

"Miss Bonner knows I have abandoned the title, but she enjoys needling me with it." The persuasive prowess of his warm voice was already beginning to put Carolyn at ease. Even Kit could feel its calming and steadying effect, while his joking reference to her removed the formality from the introduction.

"Welcome to North Dakota...Mr. Talbot," Carolyn offered in a more natural voice. "Have you been here before?"

"This is my first visit. I arrived only yesterday."

Only yesterday, Kit thought. That seemed impossible. The waitress came with their food. The conversation was interrupted until she left.

"I don't want to keep you from your lunch," the blonde said, preparing to take her leave of them. "It was nice meeting you...Mr. Talbot."

"It was my pleasure," he returned with another flash of that virile smile.

A tentatively friendly smile was on Kit's face when Carolyn turned to her. "It was good seeing you again, Carolyn."

"For me, too." Her gaze slid briefly to Reese then back to Kit, and a glow of happiness radiated from the blonde's face. "Oh, Kit," she breathed with barely contained fervor, "you must be so happy to have the ba—Mr. Talbot here. I mean, after all this time, you finally get to meet—"

The temperature at the table dropped to below zero as Kit withdrew behind a frigidly cold mask that froze the rest of the sentence on Carolyn's tongue. Immediately she was contrite. "Kit, I'm sorry." Her cheeks flushed a cherry pink. "I didn't mean anything by—"

"It's quite all right." Kit sliced across the apology, feeling Reese's gaze narrowing on her in sharp question. "I'll see you around sometime, Carolyn."

It was a dismissal that couldn't be ignored. "Yes, all right, Kit," the blonde murmured uncomfortably. "Goodbye."

With the departure of her former classmate, Kit avoided looking at Reese as he sat down in his chair. A pulse was hammering in her throat at his continued silent study of her and she sought to dispel some of his curiosity.

"I have no use for people like that," Kit announced, her husky voice brutally callous. "Just look." Her brown eyes flickered disdainfully over the dining room and the few heads that had begun to turn in their direction, the rumor of Reese's identity already reaching them. "Soon they'll be fawning all over you just like Carolyn. Just because you have the right to the title of baron, they think you are different. Since you are supposed to have blue blood running through your veins, it makes you something other than human." Vigorously Kit shook the salt shaker over her home fries. "This little episode just proves I'm right. You are going to have a horde of applicants for the housekeeping job."

"I think you are being hard on Mrs. Quinlan." His criticism held a cynically amused ring. "She seemed to be a very pleasant young woman. Your introduction of me took her by surprise.'

"And if she had known who you were before she came over, she would have been prissying around here like a handmaiden," Kit retorted.

"You certainly can't be accused of behaving like that around me, can you?"

"No, I can't." Briefly she met the speculative gleam in his eye before redirecting her attention to her plate of food.

"I wonder why she thought you would be so overjoyed to meet me?" Reese mused.

"Probably because she was." Kit shrugged dismissively. "Since I was raised on the Flying Eagle she expects me to be impressed when the owner, a real, live baron, condescends to pay the ranch a visit."

"Your friend obviously doesn't know you very well," he suggested dryly.

"No, she doesn't. And Carolyn isn't my friend. She is merely someone I went to school with."

"I wonder if anyone knows you very well."

"I do," Kit returned calmly and picked up her sandwich.

Their conversation came to a standstill as both directed their attention to the meal. They had barely finished when the waitress stopped at their table, a steaming coffeepot in her hand.

"More coffee?" she inquired cheerfully.

"Please," Reese nodded.

"How about dessert?"

"Nothing for me, thank you," he refused.

"I'll have some French-fried vanilla ice cream," Kit requested without hesitation.

A dark eyebrow shot up. "Some what?"

"French-fried vanilla ice cream," the waitress repeated with a knowing smile.

"I am going to have to ask the obvious." Again Kit witnessed the potentially devastating charm of his smile directed at someone else as Reese looked at the waitress. "What is it?"

"It's a large scoop of vanilla ice cream dipped in cinnamon and nutmeg and rolled in Rice Krispies, then dropped in the French fryer for a few seconds. Then it's smothered in hot fudge and topped with whipped cream," she recited by rote. "It's really very good, baron. You should try it."

The use of his title revealed how quickly the word of his presence had got around in such a short time. A smile played with the corners of Kit's mouth as she met his wry glance in her direction.

"Sounds delicious, but I'll just stay with coffee," he refused.

"Yes, sir." She refilled his cup and deftly

cleared the dishes from the table. Before she left, the waitress beamed with a bright smile. "If you change your mind about dessert, just let me know."

Reese merely nodded and Kit didn't bother to comment aloud on the change in their waitress's behavior. She had been conscientious before, but now she was doubly so. In record time the dessert was set before Kit. As she dipped her spoon into the thick fudge, Kit heard his low chuckle.

She glanced up with a challenging frown. "What's so funny?"

"You have no idea how incongruous you and that dessert seem—" mocking laughter glinted in his eyes "—like a ruthless gunfighter walking into a saloon and ordering milk."

"Why?" Kit stiffened, certain that somehow or another he had discovered a weakness in her armor.

"Enjoying rich food like that is a sensuous thing," Reese explained in a soft, taunting voice. "It doesn't fit with the image of a tomboy grown into a man-talking female that I've seen. It suggests that beneath that hard exterior exists a very sensual and passionate creature."

Her toes seemed to curl inside her boots at the way he was looking at her. His intimately suggestive gaze was roaming over the patrician fineness of her features, their natural, wholesome beauty minus the artifice of makeup. It traveled down to the man's cotton shirt Kit wore. The shapeless cut of the material could not conceal the rise and fall of her breasts as her breathing became agitated by his unnerving inspection. Kit had to look away from that bright light gleaming in his eyes.

She bent her head to stare at the dessert. "What nonsense!" she dismissed his suggestion, but she had lost her taste for the dessert and had to eat it mechanically, her usual relish for her favorite dessert banished by his penetrating comment.

It was with relief that she finished, the ice cream sitting heavily in her stomach. Reese downed the last of his coffee and looked pointedly at her.

"Are you ready?"

"Whenever you are," Kit agreed, regarding him with a chilling expression. If it was possible, she disliked him more at that minute than she had at any other time in their short acquaintance. He was a much more dangerous adversary than she had first suspected. And she also suspected that however short his visit might be, it would still be too long.

Kit rose from her chair when he did and walked with free-swinging strides to the side entrance door, while he paid for their luncheon. Theirs was a somber silence on the return trip to the ranch, with a sidetrip to the service station to pick up the repaired tire, as if both were reevaluating the situation.

CHAPTER FOUR

TWO MORNINGS LATER Kit was walking from the
barn carrying a pail of warm milk, fresh from the
cow, in her hand. The sky was blue and the sun
was bright; a summery day stretched before her.
The slamming of the screen door swinging shut at
the Big House made her stride falter slightly, but
she continued on without glancing around. She
didn't need to look to know it was Reese Talbot
who had walked out onto the outer veranda.

"Kit." His voice commanded her acknowledgment.

Since the trip into town Kit had made certain
that any encounters with Reese were kept to the
minimum and of short duration. It seemed the
easiest way to deal with the situation. This resolve
held firm as she altered her course toward the Big
House. She stopped at the corner of the house,
looking up to the porch where Reese stood.

"Was there something you wanted?" she questioned in a smooth, unemotional voice.

"What are you doing this morning?" He stood
in the sunlight, his hands on his hips in quiet
authority.

"I'm riding out to the west pasture to check on the herd," Kit answered, feeling safe that she was occupied and couldn't be volunteered to assist him.

"Good." He nodded crisply. "I'll ride along with you and take a look around myself."

Momentarily taken aback, Kit protested, "But Nate took you on a tour of the ranch yesterday."

"In the truck. I want a closer look," Reese stated.

Irritation seethed at her inability to avoid his accompaniment. "Whatever you say," she offered in tight-lipped agreement. "I'll take the milk to the house then get our horses saddled. It'll be about fifteen minutes."

"That's fine."

Kit started to turn away, then stopped. "Our horses aren't exactly what you would classify as gentle mounts. Can you ride?"

"Yes." He seemed amused by her question.

"The sun might get hot so you'd better wear a hat," she added.

"I am not a complete greenhorn, Miss Bonner," Reese drawled.

"I just thought I should warn you," she said stiffly and turned away.

He was so damned complacent, she thought angrily, so arrogantly certain that he knew everything. How she would love to take him down a peg or two! A wicked gleam brightened her dark eyes as she slowed her steps toward the house.

Kit glanced toward the shed a few yards away where Lew, Frank and Kyle were. All three of them were crouched around the tractor, still trying to complete the repairs and get it in running condition.

"Lew?" She called to the senior of the hands. When he glanced up, Kit motioned him to her.

He straightened from his crouching position by the tractor and walked over. "I think we just about got it," he declared with satisfaction.

But Kit's thoughts weren't on the tractor. "Talbot wants to ride out to the herd with me so would you saddle my bay and catch Dusty for Mr. Talbot?"

Lew's mouth dropped open and stayed that way for the span of several seconds. "You don't want Dusty," he protested. "Not for the baron."

"Yes, I do," she insisted with a feline curve to her mouth.

"But Frank—" he motioned to the older cowboy beside the tractor "—just finally caught him the other day. He's been runnin' wild all winter and you know what he's like after that. It takes a week's worth of ridin' just to get the humps out of his back."

"Yes, I know," Kit purred.

"He'll throw the baron sure as hell the first time he steps into the saddle," Lew breathed.

"Talbot assured me he wasn't a greenhorn and that he could ride."

"And you're going' to—" He saw the glint in

her eye and the look of astounded protest slowly faded into a smile that spread across his whole face. "It's goin' to be a sight to see, isn't it?" Lew chortled softly.

"It certainly is." Kit grinned.

"I'll saddle 'em and bring 'em both up to the Big House," he promised.

"Meet you there in ten minutes," Kit said and started for her own house, a new spring to her step.

Exactly ten minutes later her boots were clumping hollowly on the wood steps leading to the porch of the Big House. She saw Lew coming from the barn leading two saddled horses. Kit could feel the excitement building within her and fought to contain it.

"Are you ready, Mr. Talbot?" she called.

"Ready." He pushed the screen door open and walked out onto the porch to join her.

Her gaze ran over him in swift appraisal, faintly surprised at how natural he looked in everyday western clothes. But clothes did not a cowboy make, Kit silently paraphrased the old saying, and turned away in case those sharp hazel eyes glimpsed something in her expression.

"Lew is bringing the horses," she told Reese.

Standing at the top of the steps, hands on her hips and nerves tingling in anticipation, Kit watched the cowboy approach. One of the two horses Lew was leading was her blaze-faced bay gelding, Reno. But it was the second that drew Kit's attention.

He was a rangy buckskin, buff-colored with jet-black mane and tail and black legs. Dusty was so named because any rider who climbed on him invariably ended up dusting the dirt off the seat of his pants. Or at least that was the case whenever he hadn't been ridden for some time, as now. Once he had been ridden regularly he became an honest, hardworking cowhorse.

The buckskin's split personality wasn't visible as Lew led him toward the house. Kit's bay walked alertly, ears pricked, the reins loose, almost crowding Lew. But Dusty was plodding along, ears drooping, seemingly half-asleep.

Over by the shed Frank looked up from the tractor, took a second look when he recognized the buckskin and straightened, touching Kyle's shoulder to draw his attention. They knew instinctively what was going on and were aware they had a front-row seat to watch the fun.

Lew kept his head down, the hat brim shadowing his face and concealing the mischievous light twinkling in his eyes. Initiating new ranch hands by giving them the roughest horse in the string wasn't uncommon, but hazing a new owner was unheard of. Only Kit would have come up with the idea and had the leadership to carry it out.

"I'll take the bay, Mr. Talbot. You can have the buckskin." She forced an air of indifference into her voice as she skipped down the steps.

Kit was almost to Lew when she realized she had received no reply and there was no sound of Reese following her from the porch. She stopped and turned. Reese was at the top of the porch steps near where she had been.

His attention was on the two men over by the tractor. Then his gaze slid thoughtfully to the buckskin standing so quietly. Briefly Reese glanced at Lew holding the reins, head averted, before finally meeting Kit's questioning look.

Had he guessed? Did he know what was going on? How could he? The questions flashed through her mind. Kit's heart was pounding in her throat. He couldn't possibly know, she assured herself grimly.

"Mr. Talbot, are you ready?" she challenged.

"Yes." He descended the steps to Kit. Nothing in his expression revealed that he suspected anything was wrong and she almost sighed with relief. Lew was holding both sets of reins and started to separate those to the buckskin when Reese approached. "I'll ride the bay," Reese stated taking the reins before Lew could stop him. "The buckskin looks too placid for me."

"No!" The strangled protest leaped from Kit's mouth. He sent her an arching look of question and she attempted to temper her reaction. "I assure you he isn't."

"Then you won't mind riding him." Reese shrugged and looped the reins over the bay's neck, moving to its left side.

"But—" Words deserted her.

With a hand on the saddle horn, he paused.

"Do you object to switching mounts? Is there some reason why I shouldn't ride the bay?"

"No...that is, I always ride him." Frustrated, Kit couldn't seem to come up with an adequate reason not to switch horses.

"This time you can ride the buckskin." Reese swung effortlessly into the saddle, indicating an expertise beyond his simple statement that he could ride. This time there was a glint of challenge in his eyes when he looked down at Kit. "Are you ready?"

Her mouth thinned into a grimly angry line. Her attempt had been thwarted. There was nothing to do now but ride the buckskin herself—*if* she could. Stiff-necked, Kit walked to where Lew stood at the horse's head.

"What are you going to do?" Lew muttered through a corner of his mouth.

"Ride him," she hissed. Pulling her hat down tight, she looped the reins over the horse's neck and noticed the way he laid back his ears. "Hold on to the bridle—tight!" Kit ordered in an under-breath so Reese wouldn't hear.

While Lew tightly gripped the headstall, she crawled slowly and deliberately into the saddle, re-fusing to even glance in Reese's direction. Kit could feel the horse's muscles bunching beneath her like a spring coiling even tighter. She adjusted the reins to the desired length and made sure she was sitting deep in the saddle. A combination of excitement, fear and challenge thudded through her veins.

Glancing at Lew, she gave a curt nod and said, "I have him."

The minute he released the bridle and stepped away, the spring uncoiled. The buckskin sprang into a series of stiff-legged jumps across the yard, giving Kit the impression she was astride a run-away jackhammer. Distantly she could hear the shouts of encouragement from Lew and Frank, but she had no idea what they were saying.

When that didn't unseat her, the buckskin switched its tactics and started sunfishing, jumping and kicking his back legs high in the air, exposing his belly to the sunlight. Kit pulled leather, but this wasn't a rodeo contest. The object was to stay on any way she could. She might have too, but the horse's straightaway line of bucking had brought them to the corral fence. With hardly a miss in his stride, he veered sharply away from the obstacle.

Centrifugal force sent Kit sailing out of the saddle as if she was diving to the ground. Instinct had her rolling almost before she hit the dirt. She ended up sitting on her bruised backside, winded, jarred and mad. Her hat was cockeyed but still on her head. Kit pulled it straight, aware of the others rushing to her side and Lew walking over to catch the now quiet buckskin.

"Are you all right?" The most hated voice of all that might have asked the question was the one Kit heard. It belonged to Reese.

"No," she snapped and scrambled to her feet

without looking at him, brushing the dust from
the seat of her pants.

"It looks like I'd better ride the buckskin,"
Reese taunted lowly. "You don't seem to be man
enough to handle him."

Kit jerked her head up to glare at him. She had a
fleeting glimpse of the wickedly twinkling light in
his hazel eyes before he turned to walk to the
buckskin. His statement infuriated her, as he had
meant it to, rubbing salt into the open wound of
her pride.

Again Lew held the buckskin, but this time it
was Reese who climbed into the saddle. Fresh
from victory, the horse leaped into action while
Kit silently but fervently rooted for the equine.
Reese seemed to be glued in the saddle.

There was a movement beside her. Kit turned to
find her grandfather among the onlookers, the
bay's reins in his hand. He glanced at her.

"Was this foolishness your idea?" Nate accused.

"Yes," Kit retorted without remorse. "I
wanted to prove he isn't as great as he thinks he
is."

"Seems to me that he's the one doing the proving," he observed.

Kit looked back to see the buckskin cantering in
a circle, humping his back. Her plan had back-
fired royally. Without saying a word she took the
bay's reins from her grandfather and swung into
the saddle.

The bay started forward and Kit checked it. She glanced at the faces of the men watching Reese and saw the glimmer of respect in their eyes. It made her defeat even more bitter to swallow. With a proud thrust of her chin she touched a heel to the bay's flanks and cantered toward the circling buckskin. More than anything Kit wanted to leave the ranch yard at a gallop, and alone.

Instead, her pride-hardened gaze met that of the buckskin's rider. "Let's go," Kit said briskly.

At a slow, rolling canter the bay left the yard with the buckskin following. They rode to the west in silence. The only sounds to break the stillness were the creaking of saddle leather, the rhythmic thud of the horses' hooves swishing through the tall grass and the trill of a meadowlark.

The terrain finally dictated a slower pace and the two horses settled into a ground-eating walk. Kit shifted in her saddle and winced at the stab of pain in her bruised hip.

"Sore?" Reese questioned.

Kit sliced him an angry look, seeing that bared smile again, a mocking curve of his mouth as he showed his teeth. The stamp of lordly arrogance was in the bluntly angled contours of his face, a knowing glitter in the gold flecks of his light brown eyes.

"Yes." And there were a lot more places that were going to hurt before the day was over.

"You're upset because I'm not the one feeling

all those aches and pains, aren't you?" he mocked.

"You guessed right away about Dusty, didn't you?" accused Kit.

"Yes."

She rode in silence for several strides, fighting the desire to defend her actions before finally succumbing to it. "It was only a bit of innocent hazing."

"I know."

Kit turned in the saddle to glare at him. "Well, if you knew, then why didn't you go along with it?"

"But I would have missed seeing you tumbling into a heap on the ground," Reese argued, amusement lacing his voice.

Turning to stare straight ahead, she simmered. "You never would have ridden Dusty if I hadn't topped him off."

"That's something you'll never know for sure, will you?" he taunted.

"You have an answer for everything, don't you?" Kit issued the comment through gritted teeth.

"I haven't come up with one for you," Reese said cryptically.

"Stay out of my private life, Mr. Talbot," she ordered in a cold, hard voice.

Kit turned the bay and urged him down the sloping face of a twisting ravine. Reese followed on his buckskin. Their ride to the floor of the can-

yon meadow was punctuated by silence. A scattering of cattle grazed on the lush grass, both Here-
ford and Angus. A pair of white-faced calves were
nearby, kicking up their heels in frolicking play.
The approach of the riders sent them scurrying
back to their mothers, tails high in the air.

Close to the center of the canyon floor Reese
drew his horse to a stop. Kit halted, also, to see
why. He was looking around him at the rich grass-
land, the sage-dotted slopes and the distant buttes
looming on the horizon.

"And they call this the 'badlands' of North Dakota," he mused.

Kit understood the skepticism in his tone because she, too, found it wildly beautiful. "The
Sioux Indian gave it its name—*Mako Shika,*
which means 'land bad.' The French fur trappers
referred to it as the 'bad lands to cross.' It probably seemed that way after the vast stretches of
gently rolling prairies. But it is nothing like the
barren and forbidding wasteland of the South
Dakota badlands."

"You've been there?" He sat easily in the saddle, a hand resting on his thigh.

"No, but I've heard other people talk about it,"
she answered, not in the least bothered that she
had been no farther than a hundred miles from the
ranch in her life. It held everything she had ever
wanted. "If you want to see some even more spectacular scenery, you should drive through the
Teddy Roosevelt National Park, north of Me-

dora." Kit was warming to a subject that she loved best—the land. "We had a cowboy from Texas work for us one year. He said he'd seen some high country before, but this was the wildest, lonesomest land he had ever known."

"He could be right," Reese agreed.

"It hasn't changed that much since the time that the Indians roamed it or when Teddy Roosevelt had his Maltese Cross ranch north of here on the other side of the Little Missouri River. The advent of the railroad brought the ranchers. The only major difference between those times and today is that instead of the longhorn cattle from the trail herds not getting fat on the grass, we have Herefords and Angus grazing on the land."

"And the buffalo and the Indians are gone," he reminded her dryly.

"Yes," Kit admitted in an offhand acknowledgment. "That's another interesting thing. The Sioux were a relatively weak tribe, driven west by the Chippewas. But when they acquired horses they became one of the most powerful Plains tribes. Some consider that they were the finest mounted cavalry the world has ever known."

"You love everything about this country, don't you? Its past, its present." Reese omitted "its future."

Kit was suddenly reminded that he owned this land. "Yes." Her voice vibrated huskily with the fierceness of her feelings. "And when you love something, it rightfully belongs to you."

"Does it?"

It was a rhetorical question, one that Reese didn't allow Kit the opportunity of offering a comment. With a touch of his heel he urged the buckskin into a canter. He was two lengths away before Kit recovered to follow suit. The distance separating them remained the same as they crossed the meadow, Reese in the lead.

The buckskin flushed a cock pheasant from a nearby bush and spooked when it flew up in front of him. The buff-colored horse lunged sideways, skittering away from the game bird. Reese's reflexes were equally swift; effortlessly he stayed firmly in the saddle despite the sudden change in direction. In control, he checked the horse's attempt to bolt.

When he had calmed it Kit had to ask, "Where did you learn to ride?" It was a compliment to his skill in the saddle, grudgingly given.

"I've been riding since I was small. English-style, western, bareback. You name it and I've tried it." The assertion was made without a single bragging note, a flat statement of experience. "I did some professional showing of hunters for my father when I was younger."

"I imagine you won him quite a few trophies." She didn't know where that bitterly derisive tone had come from.

"A few," Reese admitted, appearing to be more interested in studying her expression than his answer.

Kit stared at a point between the bay's ears, her eyes feeling almost arid. "I suppose he displayed them in his castle."

His mouth quirked. "To my knowledge, we never had a castle in Maryland."

"In Maryland?" Kit repeated in sharp surprise and confusion. "But the baron...was he your grandfather?"

"No, he was a distant relative of mine. His grandfather and my great-grandfather were first cousins, I think," he explained. "When the baron died without an heir, I was the closest living relative, which shows you how much the family has died out."

"I see," she murmured stiffly. "And you are from Maryland?"

"Yes, I was born there. My father worked for the British foreign service in the diplomatic branch. Actually I have dual citizenship, but I consider myself an American."

"I presume your parents are dead?"

"Yes, I'm an orphan, like you, only much more recently," Reese stated, patiently answering her questions. "My parents were killed in a plane crash ten years ago."

"What did you do? Or what do you do for a living?" Kit eyed him thoughtfully.

There was a cynical twist to his mouth. "My parents were fairly wealthy so I have enjoyed the privilege of not having to do anything for a living. I've dabbled in many things and traveled a lot."

He didn't sound proud of it. In fact, Kit thought he seemed bored.

"And your home is in Maryland?"

"I don't have a home."

"You must have an unusual wife," Kit observed.

Reese cast her a mocking look. "Are you asking if I'm married?"

"Aren't you?" she countered.

"Have you seen any evidence of one?"

"If you mean because she didn't come with you, I am supposed to assume that you don't have one, I haven't. This ranch has a history of not being liked by the wives of its owners. Their visits have been even rarer than those of their husbands," Kit retorted.

"In this case, I don't happen to be married. A wife has always been in the same, confining category as property and I've made it a point not to acquire either."

His reply caused Kit to jerk at the reins, halting her horse, her eyes widening. "Then what about the ranch? Are you going to sell it?"

He stopped his horse, leveling a look at her slightly anxious expression. "I haven't made up my mind."

Her jaw tightened. "I don't see how you could even consider selling it."

"I haven't said I would." A dark eyebrow lifted at the anger in her words, finding her defense of the ranch amusing. "It might be a good investment. And—" his gaze swept the ruggedly beautiful landscape "—it could make a pleasant retreat for a few months of the year." His gaze returned to dwell lazily on Kit. "What's the matter? Are you afraid if I sell it that the new owner might not keep you on?"

"No," Kit answered with calm certainty. "I'm not worried about that."

Reese was curious and skeptical. "You aren't concerned that you might lose your home if I sell out?"

"No matter what you do I won't leave the ranch," Kit stated flatly and nudged her horse forward to end the conversation.

CHAPTER FIVE

"HE SAID HE MIGHT SELL." Kit wrapped her wet hair in a towel and turned to her grandfather. "Do you think he will?"

It was more than two weeks since Reese had brought up the possibility that he would dispose of the ranch. Despite her declaration that his sale wouldn't affect her, there were certain aspects of it that would.

"I don't know. He could." Nate didn't glance up from his newspaper.

"Has he said anything about it to you?"

"He doesn't confide such things to me," he answered. "It isn't likely he'll discuss it until he makes up his mind one way or the other. Either way it makes no difference to us."

"I know."

The house they lived in and two acres around it did not belong to the ranch so neither Kit nor her grandfather were concerned about having to leave their home after all these years. She had guessed by his question that Reese Talbot wasn't aware that his predecessor had deeded it away and she hadn't bothered to inform him of it.

Her grandfather's absorption in the paper drew a sigh from Kit as she turned away. Inexplicably restless, she moved toward the back door and the pleasantly cool night air blowing in to stir the long cotton robe against her bare legs. The day had been hot, and despite a shower and shampoo Kit still felt a bit sticky. Her hair needed to be dried, but the towel would absorb a lot of the wetness and the rest could be done later.

"Nate, I'm going outside for a walk," she called to her grandfather and received an incoherent murmur of acknowledgment.

Pushing open the screen door, Kit walked out into the night. Overhead, there was a skyful of stars and a smiling moon. The towering cottonwoods along the Little Missouri formed black cobwebs against a dark landscape. Crickets were singing in the grasses, hopping away in silence when Kit strolled near. The air was heavy with the scent of new hay and she inhaled the pungent fragrance in contentment.

The first cutting was all stacked for next winter's use, a wearying job even with modern machinery. Reese had surprised Kit by helping with the cutting, proving he wasn't averse to physical labor. If he had suffered from sore, stiff muscles he hadn't let on. With no small degree of cynicism Kit thought that he'd found the demanding work a change from his normal routine. A steady diet of it would probably soon wear thin.

Thoughts of him were too disquieting on such a

peaceful night. The slight breeze was cooling, the prickling of warmth on her skin already easing under its caress, the cotton robe unbuttoned at the throat. A rustling of the grasses warned her that she was not alone and Kit turned toward the sound.

"It's a beautiful night, isn't it?" Reese commented.

"Yes, it is," Kit agreed smoothly and resumed her strolling pace with Reese falling in step beside her. "That's one of the nice things about summer here. The days may be hot, but the nights are usually pleasant."

"Is there anything you don't like about this area?" he jeered softly.

Your presence here, she could have said, but didn't. "Very little," Kit admitted instead. Her wandering path was making a full circle, directing her back toward her house.

"Are you trying to sell me on the idea of keeping this ranch?"

She couldn't see his face very well in the dimness of the moonlight, but she could feel his eyes watching her. "Would it do any good if I tried?" she asked.

"None at all."

"And have you decided whether you are going to keep the ranch or not?" Since he introduced the subject, Kit saw nothing wrong with pursuing it.

"No." Reese sounded impatient, as if he regretted bringing up the topic.

"You brought it up. I didn't," she reminded him needlessly.

He ran his gaze over her, taking in the long cotton robe and the towel wrapped in a high crown around her head. "You remind me of a high priestess with that towel on your head," he observed in a lazy drawl.

"Do I?" He had changed the subject and Kit had no interest in any other conversation. She made a slight alteration in the course of her path to make a more direct line to the house.

"Saturday night and no date. That must be a sad state of affairs for a young woman." The thread of mockery running through his voice played like an irritant over her nerve ends.

"Not at all," Kit denied with a faintly haughty lift to her chin. "I prefer it that way."

"Do moonlight strolls ease that restless frustration of forced celibacy?" Reese taunted.

Her features hardened into a palely golden mask as she shot him a cold look. "I came out for a breath of fresh air, but it's become a bit suffocating out here. So if you'll excuse me, I'll turn in." Kit quickened her step, catching the flash of white and hating him and his silent laughter.

The heel of her slipper caught the hem of her robe and tripped her. Kit stumbled forward. A muscled arm hooked the side of her waist to catch her and pull her to the steadying length of his body. The shock of the near fall and the sudden contact with his hard male shape momentarily froze her into stillness.

Her hipbone felt the pressure of his muscular thigh. His fingers were spread over the curve of her waist, extending to the lower edge of her rib cage. The unfamiliar touch of a man's hand seemed to burn through the thin fibers of her robe, throwing her senses into a turmoil that Kit rejected violently.

"I'm all right. Let me go," she ordered in a vibrantly husky voice.

"Of course," Reese acquiesced without hesitation.

The arm around the back of her waist loosened its hold. As his hand fell away from her waist it made an absent and light exploration of the curve of her hip and the firm roundness of her buttocks. Kit jerked away, her skin tingling through the material where he had so intimately and indifferently felt her. She blamed the rising heat in her cheeks on anger at his liberties with her person.

Reese seemed aware of what he had done and Kit muffled her indignant reaction to offer a frigid "Good night, Mr. Talbot." She turned toward the porch steps to her home.

His voice pursued her. "Who did this to you, Kit?" he asked quietly and curiously. "Who hurt you?"

His questions stopped her, but she didn't turn around. "I don't know what you are talking about." She injected an even cooler temperature in her reply.

"Was it a man?"

A bitter, choked sound like laughter came from her throat. "Yes, you could say that."

Before Reese could make any further inquiries, Kit hurried up the steps. The light streaming from the back door briefly silhouetted her feminine shape, changing the cotton material of her robe to gossamer. Then she was inside, the screen door slamming.

IT WAS AN EPISODE that Kit couldn't so easily close her mind to. Its memory came back many times in the following ten days, its revival marked by each time she saw him. Her only means to combat it was to be harder and colder toward Reese than before.

With long, impatient strides Kit crossed the ranch yard toward her house. It was well past one o'clock, nearly two. The sun was high and hot overhead and her stomach was rumbling. She had been too busy at lunchtime to eat. Perspiring from the heat, and hungry as well, Kit hurried toward the house, hoping a quick snack would take the edge off this feeling of irritability.

"Miss Bonner? Kitty?"

The sound of a female voice brought her up short and she turned toward the Big House and the middle-aged woman standing on the porch, Mrs. Kent, a widowed lady Reese had hired to take care of the house and his meals. Kit still hadn't gotten used to having a woman around the strictly male-oriented ranch.

"Yes, Mrs. Kent, what is it?" Her demand was abrupt; she was anxious not to be delayed.

The woman smoothed a hand over her plump, aproned figure, betraying an inner nervousness. "Have you seen Mr. Talbot?"

"No, I haven't," she was glad to say.

"Oh." The answer plainly didn't please the pepper-haired woman. "I thought he might be with you."

Frowning, the housekeeper lifted her gaze to the south where the windbreak of trees didn't obstruct the view of the ranchland.

"He isn't. I haven't seen him at all today," Kit enlarged on her previous answer. Mrs. Kent's behavior forced her to ask, "Why? What's wrong?"

"He left shortly after breakfast this morning and said he'd be back for lunch, but I haven't seen a sign of him." She looked back to Kit. "I'm getting worried."

Compressing her lips into a thin line, Kit breathed in deeply. "Did he say where he was going when he left this morning?"

"I thought he mentioned something about going for a ride."

Kit made a sweeping inventory of the yard. Reese's car was there and so was one of the pickups. She had just seen Frank by himself in the other truck so that eliminated the possibility Reese had taken one of the vehicles.

"Is he maybe with one of the others?" Mrs. Kent asked hopefully.

"No." Kit had seen all three of the hands within the last hour and a half. Reese had not been with any of them. Her gaze searched over the horses in the corral next to the barn. The buckskin was missing and she knew Reese had taken to riding him. "Damn," she cursed under her breath.

"What do you think we should do?" The housekeeper's anxiety increased as each possibility was cast aside.

Kit didn't answer immediately, looking to the wild land where a landmark could disappear in a maze of others of similar shape. Reese had said he was going riding and the buckskin was gone. Knowing the vagaries of his mount, it was possible he had been thrown. Even the best riders can be bucked off. But Kit was convinced that it was more likely he had ridden too far and become lost in the bewildering terrain.

"I'll go out and look for him," she said with decision. "Tell Nate what's happened while I saddle a horse. He can take the truck and go look for him. If we aren't back with him by the time Lew and the others show up, you'd better send them out, too."

With a bribing pail of oats, she caught the bay gelding and saddled him with a swift economy of movement. As she rode into the yard her grandfather was just climbing into the cab of the pickup. Kit paused to speak to him, splitting up the directions they would take to widen the search for Reese. Little more than that was said.

Getting lost was serious business in this wild country.

The gnawing hollowness in her stomach was forgotten as Kit rode out. She kept to the ridges, bluffs and mesas, the places where her view was expanded by the vantage of height. She pushed her mount to cover as much territory as possible. The bay lathered up quickly in the heat of the afternoon, but he was game.

Kit, too, felt the effects of the heat. Perspiration trickled down her spine and formed a rivulet in the hollow between her breasts. The cotton shirt clung to her sweat-damp skin, hugging closely to her curves. There was a salty taste to her lips and the pungent aroma of hot horseflesh assailed her sense of smell.

For well over an hour Kit searched fruitlessly, her eyes straining at the sight of each dark shape on the land only to have it turn out to be a cow or a boulder-sized chunk of scorialike rock that had tumbled from a cliff face. The sun was brilliant even beneath the wide, shadowing brim of her hat.

On the point of a bluff Kit turned the bay to send him down a gentle slope dotted with rain pillars, tablelike pedestals of sandstone that the underlying sediment beneath the hard rock had eroded by wind and weather. Her peripheral vision caught a glimpse of movement to the far left. Kit reined in the bay and stared at the point where she thought she had seen something.

A narrow valley was formed by two ridgebacks.

Willows and young cottonwoods followed the winding path of a creek bed through its center, a creek that the summer's heat had probably reduced to a mere trickle. It was in those trees that Kit thought she had detected movement. The horse's side heaved beneath her, glad of the short rest.

A few seconds later her patience and alertness were rewarded. Reese came riding out of the trees on the buckskin. Relieved satisfaction washed through her at having found him. It didn't last long. The sight of him riding along so calmly as if he didn't have a care in the world filled her with a seething anger.

Kit reined the bay to the left and urged it down the steeper slope. A patch of loose shale clattered noisily beneath his hooves, attracting Reese's attention. Kit gave the bay his head as he slid and lunged down the hill to the other horse and rider.

Reese glowered at the sight of the lathered neck and flanks of the bay. "What do you think you're doing riding a horse that hard on a day like this?" His harsh voice slashed across her already irritable nerves.

"Is that all you can say when we've been turning this ranch upside down looking for you?" Rage quivered through her voice. "Of all the stupid, greenhorn stunts to pull, you had to go and get yourself lost!"

"Lost?" He seemed to relax indolently in his

saddle, amusement twitching around his mouth. "I'm not lost."

"What do you call it then?" Kit challenged.

"I was just doing a bit of exploring on my own."

"Is that why you didn't turn up back at the Big House for lunch today, the way you told Mrs. Kent you would?" She didn't spare the sarcasm.

"Is that what this is all about?" Reese looked surprised—in a mocking sort of way. It did little to appease Kit's temper.

"Yes, that's what all this is about!" she snapped. "The poor woman was half out of her mind when you didn't show up! Nate is out along the river looking for you. And by this time the boys have joined in the search, as well!"

"I did tell Mrs. Kent I'd be back in time for lunch," he admitted unremorsefully. "When the noon hour came around I wasn't hungry so I didn't bother to go back. It never occurred to me she'd be alarmed."

His bland indifference to the furor his absence had caused caught at the breath in her throat. It was soon expelled in a rush of abuse.

"Of all the arrogant, insensitive excuses, that has to be the worst. Let me set you straight on a few things, Mr. Talbot," Kit raged, fire blazing in her dark brown eyes, animating her usually frozen features. "When someone doesn't show up when he says he is going to, it *is* a cause for alarm around here. And when that someone is also unfamiliar with the lie of the land, the cause for alarm becomes more real. This isn't a friendly land, especially to those who are unaware of its dangers.''

"Your point is well taken, Kit,'' he acceded.

She was much too angry to notice the leisurely way his gaze was roaming over her, taking note of the way the man's shirt revealed the definitely female curves beneath it and the agitated movements of her breasts in rhythm with her breathing. The flush of anger in her cheeks gave an attractive vibrant glow to her skin.

"Is that all you have to say?'' Only in the broadest sense could his response be termed an apology.

"No.'' With an unconscious, masculine grace, Reese swung out of the saddle. "I think we should walk for a while and give you and your horse a chance to cool off.''

It was on the tip of her sharp tongue to inform him that she had no desire to cool off, but a glance at the shiny, wet neck of her horse stopped it. The bay did need a breather after the way she had pushed him in her search for Reese.

As he moved to the head of her horse, Kit placed a hand on the saddlehorn and started to swing a leg over the saddle. His hands gripped the sides of her waist and Kit stopped, standing in the air with one foot in the stirrup. Twisting to glare at him, she leaned against the saddle skirt.

"I have been getting on and off horses by my-

self for years. I don't need your help!'' she lashed
out angrily.

A steely glint entered his eyes. "That's too bad,
because you are going to get it."

His fingers bit into her flesh to increase his
hold. Kit swung at his arm, in too precarious a
position to offer more than a brief resistance.
Already he was lifting her clear of the saddle as if
her slender body weighed no more than air. Her
feet touched the ground and she tried to wrench
away from his hands, hitting at him and kicking.

With consummate ease Reese turned her
around, a muscled arm across the middle of her
back crushing her to his length. Her arms were
pinned against his chest and Kit knew she was
trapped by his superior male strength. Immediately she ceased struggling to hold herself rigidly still
in his grip. Adrenalin surged through her system
and her heart beat wildly in rage at her impotence.

Tipping her head back she glared at the aggressive lines of his face, complacently male and
cynically amused by her struggles. Her chin jutted
forward at a belligerent angle, her jaw hard and set.

"I'm on the ground. You can let me go." Kit
issued the order through savagely clenched teeth.
The heat of his body, so hard and unyielding, was
making itself felt and she didn't like the sensation.

There was a dangerous glint in his eyes as if he
enjoyed having her at his mercy. His gaze lifted a
few inches, that arrogant and rough half smile
playing with his mouth.

"Do you know I've never seen you without that damned hat?" The low, huskily amused sound of his voice seemed to come from deep in his throat.

His words registered with a flash of warning. But other than a strangled "No!" there was nothing Kit could do to stop him before he had tugged the weathered brown hat from her head and a cascade of chestnut gold hair tumbled about her shoulders.

"Well, I'll be damned." There was a chuckle in his murmur of surprise as he wound his fingers into the silken strands shimmering with highlights of liquid gold in the sunshine.

"Stop it." Kit tried to twist away from his touch, straining against the iron band of his arm across her back, and closing her eyes against the feel of his hand running through her hair.

"Why haven't you chopped it off like a boy?" Reese mocked, but with a thread of curiosity.

"Because," she breathed out heavily, frustrated and unable to cope with the situation, "it's too much trouble getting it cut all the time."

"Is that the real reason?" he taunted skeptically.

"Yes!" Kit flashed, her eyes snapping open with bitter recrimination for doubting her words.

Something in his hooded look paralyzed her. A shiver ran down her spine as she felt the hard, vibrant intention of his body. His attention had shifted to her lips. Instantly Kit stiffened and would have renewed her struggles. But a fistful of hair tugged her into motionlessness and Kit was helpless to elude his mouth, descending with deliberate slowness.

"No," she moaned against the touch of his male lips against hers, but it came out muffled and completely unheeded.

Their touch was firm, faintly ravaging in their exploration of her softness. She closed her eyes, trying to shut out his image and the awareness of the solid flesh of a man's body molded to hers. Relentlessly he plied the sweetness of her lips, dominating, mastering and driving out all other thought but his possession. The heat of the afternoon seemed to intensify the hot, male odor of him, smothering her breath as well as all other smells.

The brilliant sun seemed to be affecting her. Kit felt dizzy and strangely weightless. With her arms pinned, her fingers clutched at his shirt front, feeling the granite wall it covered. Something warm and urgent was being unleashed inside her and Kit fought it, whimpering in her throat like a child at this unknown quality she didn't understand.

Immediately at the sound, the locking hold of his arm around her seemed to relax, as if Reese believed he had conquered her. With a quick, frightened twist she was out of his arms, turning away to push the tousled disarray of tawny brown hair away and conceal her expression with her hand. Kit was more shaken by the kiss than she cared to admit.

"You are full of surprises," Reese declared in a husky, mocking tone. "It looks as if there's some truth in that saying about letting your hair down."

Her back was to him and his hands settled caressingly on her shoulders, his warm breath fanning her hair an instant before Kit stepped away, shrugging free of his touch.

"Don't be too sure about that." Thankfully her voice was fairly steady even if her heart was still thudding erratically in her chest.

"Admit it, Kit." He made no further move to approach her. "That hard shell of yours cracked. Maybe I should have peeled it away layer by layer."

"Better men than you have tried." She turned to face him, confident she had regained enough of her composure to battle him.

"Bold words," Reese insisted with a knowing glitter in those unsettling hazel eyes. "And lies. I tasted the inexperience of your lips. Not that many men have tried."

Her gaze faltered for an instant. "That's what you think."

"That is what I *know*," he stressed softly. "I doubt if your experience goes beyond a few stolen kisses behind the barn. I'd swear you never made it to the hayloft."

She drew herself up to her full height, summoning all her pride to not be intimidated by the way he towered so closely before her. "Is that something I should be ashamed about?" Kit challenged.

"No, on the contrary." Lazily he reached out, his fingers closing around the shirt button nestled in the vee of her breasts. "Every man likes to be the first."

Trembling in a white-hot rage at the intimate brush of his hand, Kit slapped it away. "You have the time and place mixed up." Her voice was raw with the fury of her reaction. "This is not the eighteenth century or jolly old England. You may be a lord but you can't take your pick of the local virgins."

His eyes narrowed dangerously, a muscle twitching along a tightened jaw. "By 'every man' I was not necessarily referring to myself. I don't go around seducing every virgin I meet. The women who come to my bed are willing. They are not taken by force."

"Women. In the plural," Kit tossed back contemptuously.

"Yes, in the plural." His voice was threateningly low. "I don't get tied down to one. And my reference to you was to indicate that the man *you* chose would be grateful for the gift."

"It will never be you!"

"That's your choice," Reese snapped. "And believe me, I'm not at all sure I'd want you."

"Good." Something was strangling her throat, making her voice tight and huskier than normal. "You just stick to dainty little blond-haired dolls that will fawn all over you, all female and subservient."

"I have never preferred blondes over brunettes
or vice versa," he said coldly. "But one thing is
sure. Whomever I make love to, it's someone who
isn't afraid of being a woman."

"Meaning I am?" she retorted.

"Meaning you are," he stated. His gaze suddenly ran over her, piercing and probing. "What
did this man do to you? The one who hurt you so
badly?"

Everything inside her seemed to freeze up at his
question. Her blood turned to icicles. Kit withdrew behind a frigid and impenetrable mask, all
emotion—even anger—frozen up inside. She per-
mitted herself to feel nothing.

Her reaction only intensified Reese's curiosity.
"What did he do to make you turn against your
own sexuality? To make you lock up all your
warm, passionate emotions inside and throw away
the key so that the next man who comes along has
to pick the lock?"

"No one asked you to come here." Deliberately
Kit ignored his questions. "Why couldn't you just
be satisfied with receiving the considerable profits
from the ranch? It was good enough for all your
other predecessors. Why isn't it good enough for
you?"

He gave her a long, considering look filled with
a cynical kind of arrogance. "You'd like me to
leave, wouldn't you?"

"Yes."

"To leave and never come back," Reese went
further.

"To leave and never come back," Kit repeated, the fervor of her wish evident despite the coldness of her tone. "And you will. Someday you will. Then everything will go back to being the way it was before you came."

"Will it?" His lip curled.

"You aren't needed here and you aren't wanted here." She tossed her head back, regal and proud. "So why don't you leave?"

"You've had your say. Now I'll have mine," he said smoothly. "I'll leave when I'm damned good and ready and not a minute before—*if* I leave at all."

Turning, Reese picked up the trailing reins of the buckskin and prepared to mount. Kit stared at him, hating him with all her might and knowing he disturbed her physically the way she had prayed no man ever would.

"How can you stay where you aren't wanted?" she demanded.

"You forget—" Reeese swung into the saddle and stared down at her "—I own this land. I don't have to be wanted to stay here." His gaze flicked to her shimmering chestnut hair. "Don't forget your hat. The sun is strong today."

Pivoting stiffly, Kit swept the hair atop her head and reached for the hat discarded on the ground. She slapped it against her thigh to knock the dust off it, then worked it over the hair piled on her head, tucking the stray hairs under the crown. The bay had wandered a few feet away. Kit caught up his reins and mounted.

"Shall I lead the way back to the ranch?" Reese questioned tauntingly. "I'd like to prove to you that I'm not lost."

"You own this place. You don't have to ask my permission," she responded bitterly.

He eyed her for a pulsing second, his expression hard and grim. Then he turned the buckskin in the direction of the distant ranch yard and took the lead.

CHAPTER SIX

FRANK JARVIS STOOD RIGIDLY before Kit, his slightly paunchy figure unmoving, a pinched whiteness about his sunburned face and a resentful glitter in his eyes despite his silence.

"When I tell you to do something I expect it to be done!" Kit continued her lashing barrage that had begun some minutes ago. "I didn't tell you to do it tomorrow or the day after. I told you I wanted it done this afternoon. Now why isn't it? What possible excuse could you have?"

"Kyle's horse had thrown a shoe," Frank began defensively. Among his other talents, which included cooking, he was also a farrier. "The sorrel had already worn his down to a nub and your bay, Reno, had one loose. And I figured that since we were done with the hayin' for a while, we wouldn't be needin' the mower right away."

"It isn't for you to decide when we need the mower!" Kit retorted. "I told you I wanted it repaired today and that is exactly what I meant!"

She knew she was being unreasonable. Even when the words came out of her mouth she knew she was being unfair. But once started, Kit couldn't seem to stop. Some horrible demon kept driving her on.

And it wasn't easy for Frank to keep taking her abuse. In the first place, like Lew, he was old enough to be her father. And he'd put his years in at the Flying Eagle, enough so that the fact that he was conscientious about his work couldn't be questioned. Worst of all, he was being dressed down by a female. For an old-fashioned type of man like Frank Jarvis, that was hard to swallow.

"It seemed to me like the horses were more important," he defended.

"We have two different ideas about what is important," Kit retaliated. "And mine is the only one that counts!"

"If you don't like the way I do things—"

"I don't like the way you do things!" Kit could have bitten off her tongue for that.

"Careful there, Kitty." A third voice joined them in the interior shadows of the barn. "If you go to firin' the cook—" it was Lew standing just inside the door "—you just might find the rest of us walkin' out."

All the fight seemed to go out of her like the air from a deflating balloon. She turned away from both of them, hiding the sudden wave of vulnerability.

"Fix the mower tomorrow, Frank," Kit asked with a tired and beaten sound to her voice.

There was a long moment of hesitation. "I will," he promised finally.

Without moving she listened to his stilted footsteps as he walked through the scattering of hay on the barn floor and his murmured exchange with Lew at the door. It slid open, then closed. Alone, Kit leaned wearily against the rough boards of an interior barn wall.

What was the matter with her, she wondered. It had been impossible for anyone to live with her this past week, including herself. She had been like this ever since that devastating encounter with Reese when he had kissed her so thoroughly, then accused her of being afraid to be a woman.

What was she trying to prove? That she wasn't a woman? That she didn't have the ordinary passionate yearnings every other woman did? But she didn't! Kit screamed inside. She had killed them—all of them! She didn't want a man, not any man, and never Reese Talbot.

Dragging her hat from her head, Kit let her hair tumble free, hoping it would ease the pressure pounding in her head. The hand holding the hat hung limply at her side. She turned to rest her back and both shoulders against the barn wall, lifting her gaze to the hayloft overhead. A stab of pain twisted her insides and Kit screwed her mouth up to hold back the accompanying sob, succeeding in keeping it to a sniffle.

A sound came from near the door. Someone was in the barn. Immediately Kit straightened, brushing a hand across her face as if donning a mask. When her gaze probed the shadows she saw Lew standing there.

"I...I thought you had gone." Her voice faltered for only a second before gaining its steadiness.

"You lit into Kyle nȯt more'n twenty minutes ago. Now Frank. I figured it was my turn next," he said, criticizing her behavior.

She lowered her head briefly. "I don't know what's the matter with me lately." It was the closest Kit could come to an apology.

"I don't know, either, but I sure hope it don't last, 'cause you got all the rest of us snarlin' at each other. This is gettin' to be a downright unfriendly place," he declared in all seriousness.

Kit knew Lew very well. None of this was the reason he had stayed behind when Frank had left. "What do you want, Lew?"

"It's not me that wants anything. It's the boss—" tactfully, he corrected that "—the baron. He wants to see you."

The mention of Reese brought every sense to full alertness; Kit was wary as a deer at the first crack of a twig under a hunter's foot. Tension crackled about her.

"Did he say why?" she questioned.

"Nope, and I didn't ask. It's been gettin' to where I don't mind nobody's business but my own around here."

Her fingers tightened on her hat, crumpling the

brim. "Tell him I'm busy," Kit snapped, turning away.

"Won't do any good," Lew answered placidly. "He said for you to come as soon as you're free."

There was no way to avoid it. "All right," she agreed in fatal acceptance. "If he asks, tell him I'll be there shortly."

After the barn door had slid shut on Lew, Kit took a few extra minutes to compose herself. Her shell had become brittle and she needed to strengthen it. There was no thought of disregarding the edict. Kit wanted to admit neither to herself nor to Reese just how much he could disturb her.

Nothing in her swinging stride nor her erect carriage betrayed that she was going to the meeting with any feeling of trepidation. Outwardly she looked completely calm and composed, on a routine errand. Inwardly Kit was filled with questions that all centered around one focal point—why did he want to see her?

Since Reese had taken up residence in the Big House, Kit didn't come and go as she pleased through its halls. A fly buzzed angrily as she rapped on the screen door and waited. Almost instantly Mrs. Kent bustled into view behind the fine wire mesh.

"Oh, hello, Miss Bonner—Kitty." The housekeeper always stumbled over her name, inevitably using both formal and informal.

Kit was accustomed to this nervousness from

people who had heard about her, and overlooked it. "Mr. Talbot wants to see me."

"Yes, he told me." She pushed the screen door open. "Come in. He's in the library."

Not that room! All her sensibilities protested, but there was nothing she could do about it. Stiffening her spine, Kit entered the house. The thick walls made the house slightly cooler and Kit had to suppress a shiver at the change.

The library door was closed and Kit paused before it as the housekeeper continued on. Her palm felt clammy as she lifted her hand to knock on the door. Immediately muffled permission to enter was given from the other side.

When Kit opened the door her gaze was unavoidably drawn to the portrait over the mantelpiece, in a direct line to the door. As always, the handsomely arrogant face had the ability to fan the flames of her hatred. It was only natural that some of it was transferred to Reese when she turned to find him seated behind the desk, appearing very much to be the lord of the manor with his aquiline features and his own brand of aggressive male arrogance.

"Lew said you wanted to see me." Kit attempted to bank the fires behind a veil of cool indifference, but the hardness of his expression made them seethe all the hotter.

"Have a seat." He nodded toward the straight-backed chair in front of his desk.

"No, thank you." At least this way she could

enjoy the rarity of looking down at him instead of always lifting her gaze.

Kit was aware of the change in his attitude toward her. Where once Reese had looked on her with mocking cynicism, there was now a callousness. She could see it in that faintly raised eyebrow above a piercing stare. There was something forbidding in the leanly hollowed cheeks and the austere line of his mouth.

"What did you want to see me about?" She wanted to get it over with and get out.

"Don't worry. It's strictly business." Amused contempt glittered briefly in his eyes.

"It never for a minute occurred to me that it might be related to anything other than the ranch," Kit replied.

The hat was still in her hand. Kit wished now that she had taken the time to put it on and secure her hair under its crown rather than leave it loose to tangle around her shoulders. She hadn't done it in an attempt to call attention to her sex.

"I've made a decision about the ranch," he announced, "and I thought you would be interested to know."

"What is it?" Kit refused to sound overly interested.

"I won't be selling it."

"Wherever your ancestors have gone to in their reward, I'm sure they'll be glad to know it's staying in the family," was her faintly biting response.

"I knew you would be overjoyed at the news."

"Is that all you wanted?"

"No, there's more," Reese assured her, leaning back in his chair with every indication that he was going to enjoy telling her. "I won't be leaving for a while, maybe not for a long while."

"That's your decision." Kit shrugged as if it didn't matter to her.

"Yes, that's my decision." He paused for a second. "When I first arrived—"

"If this is going to be a long speech I'd rather not hear it," she interrupted.

Aware of the portrait observing this scene from its canvas mat, Kit felt the tension mounting, her nerves snapping one by one under the building pressure. Soon they would all break.

"When I first arrived here—" Reese continued as if she hadn't spoken at all, and Kit tossed her hat on the corner of his desk and jammed her fingers into the back pockets of her Levi's "—I didn't interfere with the running of the ranch," he completed his sentence. "I sat back and observed what was going on. That first day when I questioned your authority to give orders to the men, you assured me that you received them from your grandfather and acted as a go-between with the men. I had no cause to doubt you."

There was a series of warning clicks in her brain. Kit knew what was coming and braced herself. There was nothing she could do except try to parry it when it came.

"Since then I've had an opportunity to see for

myself that your grandfather's management of the ranch is haphazard at best. He has become nothing more than a figurehead. You have been the driving force on this ranch."

It wasn't lost on Kit that he had used the past tense, but she kept it from showing. Maintaining her air of indifference, she returned his steady look.

"Why are you telling me this? If you aren't pleased with the way Nate is running things, you should speak to him."

"I chose to speak to you first," Reese said at his autocratic best, "because I think you know your grandfather's period of usefulness on this ranch is over."

"So he's through, is that it?" Kit challenged. "You're firing him and you expect me to back you up."

"I expect you to admit the truth of what I'm saying."

"You've given no thought at all to the years— the lifetime he has spent taking care of this ranch. You have no appreciation at all for his honesty," Kit attacked him. "He could have robbed this place blind and been justified. Is this the thanks he gets? You come along and decide he is no longer useful. He's just an old man so you want to boot him out."

His mouth thinned impatiently at her accusations. "I was thinking in terms of retirement with an adequate pension."

"How typical!" She scoffed at him with her laughter. "Pension off the old family retainer with no thought at all about what he's going to do with his empty days. Just put the old horse out to pasture. You don't care whether or not he misses the harness. Is that the way you are going to repay his loyalty?"

"What about his pride?" Reese flared. "Would Nate want me to keep him on out of pity?"

"No! Never pity! Never from you!" Kit heard herself shouting and turned abruptly away from the desk, straining to control her temper.

"Then that settles it." He, too, made an effort at control.

"Now that you've dispensed with Nate, what about me?" She walked to the fireplace hearth, trying to avoid looking at the eyes of the man in the portrait, and intensely aware of those boring into her back.

"Since I am staying and your grandfather is leaving, I can't believe that you will want to remain," he said finally.

"That's what it all comes down to, isn't it?" Kit declared. "The reason you are getting rid of Nate is to get rid of me."

"I think we both knew it would come to this," Reese stated. "We have known since the first time we met. The incident last week simply clinched it."

Kit started to smile. Her back was to him so Reese couldn't see her expression. "How soon are you expecting us to leave?"

"There's no rush. Whenever it proves convenient."

"How magnanimous of you." The smile was spreading, the satisfaction she would soon have searing through her veins.

"You won't have to worry. I'll make sure the pension is more than adequate."

Kit turned to face him, a feline purr to her voice when she spoke. "And what if I told you we can be off your property in five minutes, Talbot?"

A guarded look entered his expression. "Is that what you are telling me?"

"All it takes is the time to walk out of this house and to my own." She could see by the brief flicker of surprise that he hadn't known. She tipped her head back to emit a throaty, triumphant laugh. "You are so anxious to be rid of me. The truth is that you never can."

His jaw tightened. "I know you are going to enjoy explaining that remark."

"It's very simple." The laughter faded from her voice as bitterness took over. "You should have checked more closely into exactly what it is that you do own. The house where I live and the two acres it sits on don't belong to you."

Reese was no longer relaxed in his chair. He was leaning forward, his hands on the desk as if any second he would pounce over the top of it and tear her apart.

"It belongs to you and Nate," he concluded.

"Yes. You see, the baron, your predecessor—"

Kit waved a contemptuous hand toward the portrait "—has already made some provisions for our future."

"How thoughtful of him."

"Yes, wasn't it?" She nearly choked on that, the galling pain inside almost more than she could bear. "So you can see how futile your efforts are to be rid of us. You can retire Nate and dispense with me, but you can't get us out of your sight."

"That's why you were so unconcerned about having to leave if I sold the ranch." The harsh glitter of his eyes never left her face.

"That's right. No matter what you do, we'll still be here—in the house just down the hill. You'll see us every day," Kit taunted. "So your grand plan to eliminate us from your life is all for nothing. It can't be done."

Uncoiling himself from his chair, Reese walked slowly around to the front corner of the desk. "How much, Kit?" he challenged.

She didn't follow his question. "What are you talking about?" she demanded coldly.

"How much do you want? I'll buy it from you. Just name your price."

The audacity that he would even think they would consider it boiled within her. "Do you think we'll sell it?" Kit blazed. "Nate brought his bride here. His daughter was born here—and his granddaughter. His wife and his daughter are buried here. Nate will be buried here and *I* will be buried here. We will never sell it!"

"Everybody has a price."

"Money isn't our god! We belong to the land. You can't buy us off. We will be here to wave goodbye to you when you leave. The land is ours!"

"You can be assured I'll do some checking on that." His look was a forbidding one. "In the meantime, it seems we have a standoff."

His checking would uncover more than a deeded title. A flame of inevitability seared through her, consuming and scorching. Her backbone became ramrod straight; her shoulders were squared, her arms held rigidly at her sides. The noble carriage of her head was part of the savage pride with which Kit armed herself, haughty and regal and protective.

"We were here before you. We will be here when you leave," Kit declared.

His brooding gaze skimmed her length. "Kyle was right...yes, Kyle," Reese commented with a cold, curling smile. "Remember an hour ago you stood before him in all your majestic anger and tore him apart. When you left I heard him call you the virgin queen. That's what you look like standing in front of the fireplace. The supreme ruler."

Something splintered inside her. "You should have waited around." Kit knew what she was saying. She wanted him to know. She wanted to lash out at him and cut him with the words that had been used on her. "You would have heard what else he calls me. What everyone has called me. The baron's bastard daughter."

The fine white rage of a million hurts trembled through Kit as she saw his gathering frown, the sudden intensity of his gaze, and the look he darted to the portrait above her head.

"He was your father?"

"Oh, I can't prove it." Kit dismissed the need with a tiny but infinitely proud shrug. "On my birth certificate the father is listed as unknown. There's little physical resemblance since I take after my mother."

"When? I—" Muscles leaped along his jaw, his mouth clamping shut as if he regretted the question.

But for Kit it was like the spewing forth of all the bottled-up hate and bitterness. She wanted him to know where once she had dreaded his finding out.

"Like you, the baron paid a visit to this ranch twenty-two years ago when he inherited. The portrait was done at about the same time, but Nate has assured me he looked older than that. He was in his forties at the time. No doubt the artist practiced flattery." Kit felt all the raging resentment and hurt when she glanced up to the painting.

"And your mother?"

"She was seventeen at the time, a young girl just blossoming into a woman, and the baron just couldn't resist aiding the budding process," Kit issued spitefully. "Her name was Sara, which the baron informed her meant 'princess.' It isn't any wonder that her head was turned by the attentions of a handsome, wealthy and titled man. He must have seemed like Prince Charming coming to carry her away to his castle."

"But surely your grandfather—" Reese frowned.

A bubble of bitter laughter came from her throat. "Nate doesn't have a snobbish bone in his body. You must remember Sara was his only child, the light of his life. Nothing was too good for her. Her happiness came above all else.

"Besides, the baron was most respectful toward her. Nate had no reason to suspect that the baron's attentions were anything but honorable. In the evenings the baron courted her like a suitor in the living room, and always under the eye of Nate and my grandmother. Nate had no cause to wonder what went on during the long horseback rides in the afternoon."

"And when your grandfather learned?"

"He was shocked, angry, shamed." Kit continued to stare at the portrait, responding to the questions and trembling with the hatred of her answers. "I'm sure all the things any father would be. You can imagine his reaction when the baron informed him he was already married."

There was a muffled curse behind her, but it merely seemed an extension of her own violent feelings. What had begun as a caustic attempt to inflict pain had become a purging. The words, the story that Kit had never uttered to anyone had to be released.

"The baron was willing to fulfill any financial obligations to Sara and her child. He was very clever. He knew he was leaving and would probably never come back. So he deeded the house to Nate and arranged for Sara to receive an income for the rest of her life, and also the child when it was born."

"And your grandfather continued working for him?" Reese demanded with a frown of disbelief in his voice.

"You must understand Nate," Kit defended him staunchly. "His first thought has always been to do what was best for his family, regardless of any personal cost. When this happened he felt guilty, as if he was somehow to blame for not foreseeing it. Here he had a home and a very good job. He was among friends and could provide for his family. I don't think his pride would have let him run away. I'm sure he thought the scandal would subside in time, but the story made such delicious gossip. It's ironic, isn't it, that in our democratic society we should be so hung up on titles."

"What happened to your mother?"

"She died within a year after I was born." A new raw edge entered her voice, exposing another of her many wounds. "She must have hated the sight of me, a constant reminder of what she had done. They say she died of pneumonia, but I know it was the shame and humiliation that she couldn't endure."

"When did you find out about. . . your father?" His voice was quiet, prompting her to continue.

"When I was little I didn't understand what parents were. I guess I thought grandparents were all anybody had, that everybody's parents were dead. Of course, my world was the ranch. Nate and Martha and Lew were the only people I knew and they protected me. When I was old enough to go to school, all that changed."

Kit glared at the portrait, vibrating like a volcano about to erupt. "Children can be very cruel. The older kids started calling me the baron's bastard. They were only repeating what they'd heard their parents say. I didn't understand what it meant but I knew it made me different from them and in a way that I couldn't change."

How it had hurt when they called her names. Kit could still vividly remember the bewildering pain their taunts caused. In the beginning she had been too young to conceal her sensitivity. Knowing they could get a reaction from her had only added to the children's malicious delight in teasing her to tears.

Two things Kit learned very quickly. Coming home in tears upset her beloved grandparents. They had explained, as much as a young child could understand, why she was different from the others. Although they had never used the word, Kit felt the shame that lay behind their voices, the sting of illegitimacy.

Secondly, she learned that if she stayed away

from the other children, it didn't give them a chance to hurt her. This aloofness, this holding herself apart from them, kept the story from dying. The children concluded that she did it because she thought she was too good for them, that she was royalty. The die was cast for the rest of her school years and Kit had built the hardened shell around her to protect herself from any more hurt.

"So that, dear cousin, five or six times removed—" the sarcasm of hate rolled from her tongue "—is the story." The remark was flung over her shoulder to Reese, but Kit's gaze remained riveted on the portrait, her hands clenched into fists with little of the raging fury within her released. There was too much of it and it had been contained too long. It was merely the hissing whistle of a tea kettle with the water still boiling inside.

"I'm not even a love child," she jeered at herself. "Just the product of that man's lust."

"The baron died without issue, Kit. You were his only child. Why didn't you contest my inheritance of his estate?" Reese questioned.

"And resurrect the whole scandal, expose it again to public ears? At the moment the knowledge is confined. If I had made a claim, it would have been spread all over the whole world. I have more compassion for Nate than that," she issued contemptuously. "He's an old man, as you said. He deserves to know some peace. Besides, you are welcome to it. I want nothing that belonged to him." Her look spat on the painting and the man it represented.

"He's the one who did this to you, isn't he? The one who hurt you," he guessed.

"Yes." At first, the positive answer was just a simple snapping sound. The second "yes!" was more strident, revealing the accumulated years of bitterness. "Yes!" The hoarse cry was an uncorking of emotions. "I hate him!" Every inch of Kit vibrated with the violent depths of the emotion and she hurled it at the portrait. "I hate him for what he did to my grandparents! And I hate him for what he did to my mother! And I hate him for what he's done to me! I hate him! I hate him!"

CHAPTER SEVEN

THERE WERE THREE VASES of Indian pottery on the mantelpiece below the portrait. The rage inside Kit exploded and she grabbed for one of them, intent on destroying the image of the man she despised so much. Her arm was drawn back to throw the vase when it struck something hard. The vase crashed from her hand into the empty cavity of the fireplace.

"I hate him!" Hoarse and raw, the denunciation came again.

With her first attempt thwarted, Kit tried again, reaching for a second vase. Reese tried to stop her, but she was a woman possessed. With the strength of ten, she fought to keep him from taking the vase from her. In the resulting skirmish Kit wrenched free, accidentally flinging the painted clay pot away. It broke atop the desk, sending broken chips scattering onto her hat.

The library door opened and an openmouthed Mrs. Kent stood in its frame. "What's going on?" she breathed, entirely sure she should not have come to investigate the crashing sounds.

Both Kit and Reese were breathing heavily,

separated only by a few feet and eyeing each other with the wariness of a pair of fighters about to come to blows again. Neither glanced away when the housekeeper spoke. Kit was still in the grip of the volcanic eruption of her rage.

"It's all right, Mrs. Kent," Reese dismissed her in clear sharp tones. "There's only one vase left."

The click of the closing door distracted him for only a split second, but it was all the time Kit needed to spin around and seize the last vase. This time she didn't even attempt to throw it at the picture. Her target was the personification of it. She held it threateningly over her head, aimed at Reese.

"And I hate you, too!" There were no tears in her eyes, not even of rage. They were dry and hard as a bone. "You are no better than he was! I hate you!"

With a vicious throw, she hurled the vase at Reese. He dodged it easily as it splintered against the far wall. Kit turned back to the mantel, but there were no more vases. She spied the fireplace poker and grabbed for it.

Before her fingers could curl around the metal handle, her wrist was caught in an iron grip and she was yanked away from her goal. Kit managed to twist her arm free and started hammering on his chest with both fists, unaware of the picture she made of a frightened, angry child.

"That's enough, Kit. Snap out of it!" A pair of hands gripped her shoulders, shaking her hard.

It had no effect. She was hauled against him, a

steel arm binding her close while fingers squeezed the back of her head, forcing it up. His punishing mouth smothered the angry sounds coming from her throat. Kit twisted and struggled but she couldn't writhe free of the steel embrace. The brutal kiss was relentless, grinding her lips against her teeth. Reese seemed intent on crushing the violence out of her. Eventually Kit had to submit.

When her resistance ended, the pressure of his mouth on hers changed subtly. Still firm, still commanding, it coaxed a pliancy from her lips. When he got it, his mouth opened moistly over hers, consuming, demanding, promising comfort for her ravaged soul. The hand at the back of her neck no longer threatened to snap it in two. It had begun to massage the taut cords in her neck, sensually rubbing away the violent tension that remained.

The arm circling her, locking her to him became less of a steel band. Seeking and caressing, his hand moved over her back and shoulders and hips, pressing her closer to the warm, hard support of him. There didn't seem to be an inch of her body that didn't feel the touch of his hand or his muscled flesh. There was something healing in that, as if he was wiping away every invisible scar thoughtless words had made.

Kit shuddered against him in relief that the unbearable pain had finally been assuaged. The shudder cast aside the last thin layer of her protective shell, exposing her utter vulnerability.

With a sweeping mastery Reese parted her lips, deepening the kiss with a passion that enflamed her senses and ignited that fiery core of her being Kit had always suppressed. The sheer wantonness of her response terrified Kit and her hands fluttered in protest against his chest.

"It's all right, kitten." His low, husky voice soothed her as he began kissing her eyes, her nose, her cheek, her brow. "God knows you have the right to hate." And he retraced his route all over again, his breath and mouth warm and moist and arousing.

And hate was the last emotion Kit was feeling. She was drowning in his kisses, in a sea of physical sensations, each wave that broke over her more devastating than the one before. The frantic pounding of her heart told her she wouldn't stay afloat for long.

"Reese, don't do this, please." She whispered her plea for his mercy. "Please. Let me go, Reese, please. Reese, Reese, Reese."

Even as she begged him with his name, Kit sought the lifeline of his mouth. Her lips clung to it desperately when she found it. The smell, the taste, the feel of him were all she could comprehend. Boneless, Kit melted against him and felt herself sinking. As long as she was wrapped in his arms, she didn't care.

Her knees touched something furry and solid, the bearskin rug in front of the fireplace. Then Reese's weight was pressing her backward, turning the rug into a bed for them to lie on. The passions raging through Kit were as animalistic and primitive as the rug.

His mouth was finding all sorts of erotically sensitive areas along her neck and throat, sending delicious shudders of desire shivering over her skin. Her fingers curled into the sensual thickness of his dark brown hair, keeping him there to continue his sensuous exploration.

His hands weren't still; intimately they caressed, supported and molded her. The pressing weight of his body was an exquisite pain to be enjoyed, his rangy, muscled length stretched above her. Expert fingers freed her shirt buttons and pushed the material aside. The way her breasts seemed to swell into mature ripeness at his touch stunned Kit, and stimulated her already heightened yearnings for total possession.

When Reese moved to kiss them, her own fingers tugged at the buttons of his shirt, finally loosening them all and sliding her excited hands over the hard flesh of his stomach and around to the flexing muscles of his back. Kit pulled him down to her, drawing his mouth back to her lips and letting their body heat fuse them together while glorying in the feel of his naked torso against hers.

Then he was pulling her arms from around him and spreading them above her head. He continued to kiss her lips and her face, but refused to let her hands roam freely over him.

"You crazy little sex kitten," Reese declared in a muttering moan against the curve of her mouth. "Do you have any idea what you are doing to me?"

Mutely Kit gave a negative shake of her head. She had no more idea what she was doing to him than she had of what he was doing to her. It was new and exciting and frightening. She lacked control and the will to acquire it.

"Kit." There was a sudden urgency in his hard kiss. "I want you. For God's sake, don't say no."

Her breath caught in her throat but she didn't say a thing. Reese read his own meaning into the silence, the white-hot flame of desire seeming to sear from every inch of him. He explored the jerky pulse in her neck. Kit's lashed fluttered in surrender, then snapped open as she became conscious of a pair of eyes watching them.

It was the pair of arrogant, blue eyes in the portrait staring down at the couple intertwined on the bearskin rug. Kit's stomach churned sickeningly. She was no better than her father. Her sense of decency, her moral standards were no stronger than his.

With a moaning cry of shame, she pushed Reese away and scrambled weakly to her feet, filled with self-disgust and self-loathing. Stumbling and gasping with pain, Kit ran to the door, deafening her ears to the startled, questioning sound of her name coming from Reese. She was through it in a flash and closing it behind her.

Her strength deserted her and she leaned against the opposite hallway wall, clutching her shirtfront closed. She sobbed at the agonizing pain, but her eyes were dry. There were no tears to cool the burning shame that seared her as hotly as Reese's touch had done.

Her escape was by no means complete. As if to remind her of it, the library door was yanked open. Reese stood there, dark and dangerous, desire still blazing in his eyes, his shirt hanging completely open to reveal the hard flesh of his golden tanned skin.

"Kit—" He started toward her.

She didn't cower, but spat at him like a cornered cat. "Don't touch me!"

Reese stopped, seeing her widened eyes with their shimmer of utter denial and her proudly defiant stance, even though she was flattened against the wall in fear. There were hesitant footsteps and the shadowy, plump figure of the housekeeper peered down the hallway. Kit knew Mrs. Kent couldn't help but see their mutual state of near undress, and quickly, if shakily, she began buttoning her shirt.

Reese flicked an angry and impatient glance at the housekeeper and took another step toward Kit. "Will you—"

"Don't come near me!" she ordered in a hoarse, raw voice. "Don't you ever come near me again!"

There was strength in her legs again and pride in

her erect carriage. She walked hurriedly to the
screen door and out onto the porch. Kit didn't
stop until she reached her house, and even then
continued straight to the privacy of her room. Her
grandfather stared after her, then looked in the direction of the Big House.

KIT SAT ASTRIDE HER HORSE, letting instinct keep
her in the saddle. Work, the ranch, the land...
that was all she needed, she assured herself, but
the aching pain inside of her echoed the call of
another need.

In the past week she had slept little, eaten less,
and driven herself harder than ever before. She
avoided the others, stayed to herself, working
from sunup to sundown. She was becoming gaunt,
hollow-eyed and bone-weary, but it was better
than feeling and remembering.

Kit hadn't spoken to Reese since she had ex-
changed those few bitter words with him in the
hallway of the Big House. Where he was concerned, she had developed a sixth sense that
warned her when he was near, giving her the time
to elude him.

Three times he had either come to the house or
attempted to approach her in the yard when others
were around. Each time she had walked away
from him, aware that it angered him and that the
others had begun speculating about her actions.
Twice he had attempted to follow her when she
rode out onto the range, but her familiarity with

the land allowed her to lose him before he could catch up with her.

There was no chance that Mrs. Kent had kept silent about what she had seen. Kit could guess what the housekeeper had assumed. Although her grandfather had become rather blind to what went on around him since his wife died, Kit suspected that he knew or guessed something had gone on between her and Reese. But he didn't question her although a couple of times she had caught him looking at her with a deep sadness in his eyes. It made her feel even cheaper and more wretched than before.

She approached the ranch yard through the concealing shelter of the cottonwoods along the Little Missouri River. The afternoon sun was casting long shadows from the buildings. Kit reined in her horse, a chestnut this time. She was giving the bay gelding a rest. Nobody was stirring in the yard.

Her timing seemed to be perfect and everyone was out. A glance at the Big House told her that even Reese's car was gone. Yet Kit was still wary and rode up to the rear of her house so the building would shield her from the view of anyone watching from the Big House.

Dismounting, she dropped the reins and the chestnut willingly began cropping the grass about his feet. Kit dragged herself up the steps to the house, marveling at how much physical abuse the human body could withstand and continue functioning with a semblance of normality.

Entering the house and walking into the kitchen, Kit stopped at the sink. She turned on the cold-water faucet and reached for a glass. It was hot and her throat was dry, her body parched. As she filled the glass she heard the creak of the rocker in the living room.

"Nate?" she called. "I just stopped by to tell you not to bother to fix me any supper. I'm going out again and it'll probably be late when I get back."

"Isn't it always?" a male voice answered dryly.

Kit froze, the water running over the top of the glass. She knew that low voice. It haunted her like a tormenting ghost. She had heard it in the whisper of the wind through the grasses or in the rippling rush of water. It came to her in the silence of sleep, warm and caressing and seductive.

Jerkily she set the glass down on the counter without easing her thirst and turned off the faucet. She didn't risk a glance in Reese's direction as she started for the door and escape. But he had already guessed what her reaction would be and was there to block her way.

"Not so fast, Kit," he warned.

Kit could lift her gaze no higher than the buttons of his shirt stretched taut against his chest. But that sight was equally as unnerving as meeting his gaze. Her hands had explored that hard muscled flesh and the finely curling hairs below his throat. Physically he destroyed her. Kit's senses remembered that rapturous devastation well.

"Get out of my way, Reese." His given name

came easily to her, but thankfully, she had trained her voice not to reveal her emotions.

"Not until we've talked."

"I don't have anything more to say to you, so please get out of my way," Kit repeated the commanding request.

"I have more I want to say to you and you are going to listen. Let's go into the living room, shall we?" Reese took a step toward her and Kit retreated instinctively. He stopped and she saw the hand at his side double into a fist. "My God, Kit," he breathed angrily. "I'm not going to attack you."

She flashed a wary look at his face and had to fight to keep from reeling from the aggressive sensuality etched in the male lines, darkened by anger. His hazel eyes blazed over her, taking in the gauntness of her slender shape and the smudges beneath her brown eyes. Her mask was firmly in place and he could see nothing of the trembling that was going on inside.

"I can't be blamed for questioning your reason for wanting to see me," she retorted.

"I came to talk. I'll accomplish it peaceably, with your permission, **or** by force without it. But don't make me touch you, Kit," he warned.

There was an elemental crackling in the air between them. Kit knew there was cause for his warning. Even now, with this cold war between them, the physical attraction ran high—on both sides, she suspected. It would never end with a simple touch and that was what Reese was telling her.

"Shall we go into the living room?" He repeated his earlier request.

Kit pivoted in compliance. "Where's Nate?" she demanded, knowing he wouldn't be there when she entered the room. And he wasn't.

"He's gone to town on an errand."

She couldn't sit down. For this meeting she would need to be on her feet, mentally as well as physically. Reese didn't avail himself of the chairs, either.

"An errand you arranged," she accused.

"Yes. I noticed that you have been making a habit of slipping into the ranch in the middle of the afternoon when everyone else is gone or working elsewhere," he admitted.

"So you found an excuse to get Nate out of here and waited for me to come," Kit murmured.

"Did you really think you could continue to avoid me?" Reese jeered.

"Obviously it was wishful thinking on my part, wasn't it?" She flashed him a bitter smile.

"Damn your coolness, Kit." The muscles along his jaw flexed in his effort to retain control of his temper.

Her legs felt incredibly weak. So much for her hope to stand up to him. She badly needed the support of a chair. Kit walked to the nearest one, sinking into it with an assumed air of one wanting to get the whole discussion over with.

"What did you want to speak to me about?" Kit draped her arms along the length of the armrest and crossed her legs, hoping to appear indifferently interested in his answer.

It had the desired effect of hardening his gaze. "As if you haven't guessed," he retorted sarcastically.

"Let me see, the last time we spoke we discussed your plans for Nate's retirement. Is that why you're here? To go over the details with me?" she challenged.

"You know damn well it isn't."

"The only other thing we talked about was your desire to buy this house and its property. Have you come to make an offer? I assure you, dear cousin, that we won't sell at any price."

"Cousin," Reese repeated with a savagely amused curl to his upper lip. "Is that what you are going to try to use to keep me at arm's length? Any blood relationship between us is down to a few corpuscles by now."

He came to stand beside the chair. Kit had to force herself not to cringe from him. She stared at her fingers playing nervously with the protective doily on the opposite armrest from Reese's side. She could feel his eyes studying her as surely as if he touched each feature of her face. In the end she could stand it no longer and pushed out of the chair to put a safer distance between. Hugging her arms about her, Kit turned to face him.

"There isn't any relationship between us, Reese. And there isn't going to be one," she stated.

"Liar." The confidence in his taunting reply shook Kit to the center of her very vulnerable core.

She turned away, hugging her arms even tighter around her. "Get to the point, Reese. Say whatever it is you came here to say and get out!"

"You've crawled back inside that shell of yours again, haven't you?" he accused in a disgusted sigh. "You had a taste of what it's like to really feel something and it frightened you."

"No, it sickened me," Kit murmured tightly.

"Would you look at me? I don't like talking to your back," Reese snapped.

Kit didn't move. She preferred it this way. She could pretend she was listening to a disembodied voice. It helped her to block out his presence to the rest of her senses.

"I said, look at me!" Her elbow was seized and Kit was spun around to meet the sorely tested patience in his expression.

She jerked away, trembling violently in reaction. "Don't touch me!" she cried, feeling the crack in her very thin and very brittle poise.

Swearing under his breath, Reese revealed his aquiline profile as he looked away to rake his fingers through the rumpled thickness of his hair. Kit felt her heart skip a beat.

"God," he muttered, "this isn't going at all the way I planned it." He turned back to her, lifting his hands to hold the air on either side of her, obeying her request not to be touched while instilling the sensation. "When you told me that story about the baron being your father, I—"

"You don't believe me. You think I was lying." Kit stiffened. "I'm sorry I can't offer you any proof, but—"

"I believe you," Reese corrected firmly.

"Now you feel sorry for me and maybe just a little bit guilty," she flashed.

"Yes, I felt sorry for you."

"Thanks," Kit lashed out at him with sarcasm, "but I don't need your pity or sympathy or compassion!"

"I understand you a lot better now. I know why you are so hard and tough, why you've buried yourself inside that shell. It makes you feel safe and protected. It keeps people from getting too close to you. And if you never let people too close, they can't hurt you."

"Please, I don't need you to psychoanalyze me," she retorted, closing her eyes, afraid of the way he was stripping away her defenses and exposing how insecure she was. "If that's all you came to say, just get out!"

"That isn't all I came to say," Reese answered. "It was quite a revelation the other day when I found the real Kit Bonner. I suspected there was a warm, loving core in you, but my expectations didn't match the real thing. I don't know for sure why you ran from the library as if you were being brutally assaulted. Whether—"

"You mean you weren't going to seduce me?"

Kit taunted, trying to combat the hot shame that flooded through her at the memory of that time.

"Damn it! Yes, I was going to make love to you!"

"Why? Because you found a love-starved little girl and thought you'd show her a bit of affection before you went on your way!" There were tears in her eyes as she shouted at him and the memory of her own abandoned behavior in his arms.

"I didn't intend for any of that to happen!" Reese shouted back. "Do you think I want to get mixed up with a crazy little hellcat like you?"

"Good! Because I think I've made it pretty plain that I don't want to get mixed up with you, either!" Kit was trembling. Everything inside her seemed to be caving in.

"That makes two of us, then, doesn't it?" His harshly narrowed gaze caught the shimmer of tears in her eyes.

A groan seemed to come from somewhere deep inside his chest. In the next second, Kit found herself a prisoner in his crushing embrace.

"You've got your claws into me good, kitten," Reese muttered against her hair, a throbbing note of desire in the sound. "I've told myself over and over again to forget about what happened. It was just a moment of passion that would have burned itself out anyway."

A sob of pain came from her throat and Reese began raining rough kisses over her throat. There was such raw ecstasy in his embrace, sweet punishment in the suffocating pressure of his arms that denied her breath. She didn't seem to need it. As if by osmosis she absorbed the vitality searing through him.

"When I see you walking around the ranch yard now in your men's clothes, I remember the soft, unbelievably feminine shape they are hiding," Reese murmured thickly, his hands exploring that very same shape with familiar intimacy. "At those times it's the closest I've ever come to actually wanting to tear someone's clothes off. You, my Kit, my kitten."

He kissed her long and hard. Kit had neither the strength nor the will to resist. She submitted to his hunger, offering him the appetizer of her lips and knowing his desire was for the main course. She felt his trembling struggle for control as he tore his mouth away and forced her head against his chest. The erratic hammering of his heart sounded as loud as her own.

"I know I rushed you the last time, Kit." His hands roughly stroked her hair. "You were such a fiery package of dynamite and you seemed to explode in my hands. I forgot about your innocence, that it was all new and frightening to you, but I promise I won't do it again. God!" His short, triumphant laugh held a ring of surprise. "I want to carry you out of here to my bedroom and keep you there for a week, a month." Reese lifted her head, cradling her face in his hand. The sensually dark and dangerous look in his eyes stole the breath from her lungs. "I need you, Kit. And you need me."

But not forever. He wouldn't need her forever. And Kit knew she would. She recoiled from the knowledge and from Reese's arms, turning her back on him and on the truth.

"I don't need you," Kit choked. "I don't need anybody."

"Everybody needs somebody in varying degrees." His hands slid around her waist, crossing in front to cup her breasts and draw her back to his masculine length.

"Don't worry, kitten." Reese nuzzled her neck. "I'm not like your father: I won't throw you to the wolves when I'm through."

A bitter sighing laugh slipped from her lips. "What will you do with me when you're through?"

The screen door slammed. It took both of them a second before either of them realized the significance of the sound. Reese was just lifting his head, his hands tightening on her waist to put Kit away from him when her grandfather appeared in the doorway from the kitchen to the living room. One look told the whole story. Kit wanted to die at the intense look of pain that flashed across his worn features. She swayed alarmingly and Reese's hands stayed on her waist for support.

"I was afraid something like this would happen," Nate said tiredly, staring at Reese. "When I saw you the first time I was afraid for my Kitty, especially when she reacted so violently to you. She usually doesn't react one way or another to strangers. I tried to pretend it was because of who you were and not because you were a very virile man. Are you in love with my granddaughter?''

There was a fractional increase of the pressure of his hands on her waist, a stiffening, a hesitation. A black, yawning mist of pain began to swim in front of Kit's eyes.

''Nothing has happened, Mr. Bonner.'' By avoiding the question, Reese had given her his answer.

Prior to Reese's remark, her grandfather had looked beaten, used up, old way beyond his years. Then a vigorous fire seemed to take possession of him.

''Nothing is going to happen, either!'' he barked. ''You sent me on a fool's errand so you could be alone with my granddaughter. Now I'll thank you to take your hands off of her and get. out of my house, or by God I'll kill you like I should have done the other time!''

It was only Reese's hands that kept her from falling into the black abyss before her eyes. When they were removed Kit felt herself slipping over the edge and gave a frightened cry, calling out as she became swallowed up.

CHAPTER EIGHT

IT WAS TERRIBLE. She seemed to be tumbling in slow motion into the black, bottomless pit. Kit struggled to stop the fall, crying out for Reese to save her, Reese who had let her go. For a second she felt his hand catch hers, then it was gone. And the terror started afresh. It seemed to go on endlessly.

Other hands reached out to her, but they hadn't the strength to help. Kit kept falling, falling. She had glimpses of Reese, but he was always out of reach, those strong, tanned hands beyond the grasp of her fingers. She could hear herself crying brokenly like a child. She never cried.

When Kit thought she would be forever lost in the swirling black void, the familiar pressure of his hand gripped hers, holding on and not letting her fall any farther. After that there was just a pleasant floating sensation that slowly and very gradually brought her to the surface.

Kit blinked her eyes and stirred. Gorgeously beautiful sunlight was streaming through the window, so glorious, so brilliant, so very different from the blackness she thought she'd never escape. A slight breeze blew away the last cob-webs. Suddenly it all seemed so crazy. Had it been a nightmare?

"Have you finally decided to come back to us?"

Kit turned her head, discovering it was resting on a pillow and she was lying in bed—her bed. Reese was sitting in a chair beside it. At the moment it seemed very natural for him to be there. When she looked at him he slipped his hand from the loosened grasp of her fingers and sat up straighter in her chair.

"What happened?" Her voice sounded funny, a little thick. "How did I get here?"

"You collapsed," Reese explained. Kit didn't think she had ever seen his broodingly male features look so gentle. "The doctor said it was a combination of exhaustion and severe strain. A couple of days of rest and quiet and you'll be fine."

Exhaustion, Kit thought. Yes, she had been working very hard and sleeping very little. But severe strain? A tidal wave of memory swamped her and Kit went white. Her grandfather had walked in and found them together in the living room. His harsh, angry voice came back with piercing clarity: "Get out of this house or I'll kill you."

"What are you doing here?" she breathed in alarm.

"I've been holding your hand for the last twelve

hours." His eyes crinkled at the corners when he smiled, something she hadn't seen happen before.

The rest of her mind was registering the time he had been sitting there. His hand, arm and back had to be cramped, but he didn't show any discomfort, although there was the shadow of a day's beard growth on his hollowed cheeks and jaw.

"But Nate—" Kit started to protest.

"—didn't have any choice in the matter," he interrupted smoothly and reached for the water pitcher and glass on her bed stand. "How about a drink?"

She bobbed her head numbly, stunned by his previous statement. Her grandfather had been adamant. She knew him very well and Nate never said anything he didn't mean.

The puzzled, doubting look was in her brown eyes when Reese moved to sit on the edge of the bed. Supporting her head with one hand, he lifted the water glass to her lips with the other.

"You became delirious," Reese explained. "The doctor gave you a sedative to calm you down, but you kept fighting it. Nate finally had to call me in so you would quiet down." He set the glass on the bed stand but remained seated on the bed, his hand braced next to her head on the pillow. "In the end I don't think Nate believed I was so depraved that I would molest an unconscious victim."

Kit flinched at his words and turned her head away, burying her cheek in the pillow. At the caressing touch of his hand on her hair she closed her eyes tightly.

His voice came softly. "That was meant to be a joke, Kit."

"Go away, Reese," she said stiffly. "I'm all right now. There's no reason for you to sit there anymore."

"Yes, I can tell you're feeling better.." He sounded impatient and grim. "You're beginning to sound like your old self again."

"Leave me alone. I don't need you anymore." Kit denied him and the emotion pulsing through her.

"All right," Reese agreed curtly. "But before I go, there's one thing I want you to know. I'm not going to let you crawl back inside your shell and hide, even if it means I have to go in there with you and drag you out. Do you understand me?"

"Go away, Reese. Just go away," she cried angrily, because it would be so easy for him to do what he said. He straightened from the bed and walked to the door. "And don't bother to come back!" Kit hurled at him as he opened it.

His only response was a twisted smile. Kit wasn't sure what that meant.

Reese had barely left when Mrs. Kent appeared, bringing some nourishing hot broth and a speculatively curious expression. The housekeeper repeated the doctor's admonition that Kit needed at least two days of complete rest and explained away her presence in the house by saying that Reese had asked her to lend a hand.

Two days of rest seemed an impossible order. However, with the aid of a sleeping pill left by the doctor, Kit practically slept around the clock the first twenty-four hours. Around noon of the following day she had been awake for a couple of hours and had eaten a light breakfast. Naturally her grandfather had been in to sit with her, but they had remarkably little to say to each other, both of them feeling the constraint of the situation.

Kit was lying in bed, trying not to think about anything, but it wasn't easy to keep her mind blank. She heard the back screen door open and close and her grandfather speak to someone. It was Reese's voice that responded. Kit tensed when she heard footsteps approaching her room, then recognized the placidly even tread as her grandfather's. It didn't occur to her to feign sleep when he opened the door.

There was no expression whatsoever on his age-lined face. "Reese is here to see you again." His choice of words indicated it wasn't the first time in the past twenty-four hours that Reese had stopped in to check on her progress. "Shall I send him in?"

Kit's answer was a sharp, negative shake of her head. When he left and closed the door, she rolled onto her side, curling up into a tight ball of pain. Nate's stoic attitude hurt worse than his anger could have.

Not once had he questioned her about Reese, never asking how involved she had become with him. Kit was too ashamed of the feelings she couldn't control to talk to Nate about them. She felt she had let him down.

Reese stopped by several times in the next two days and every time Kit refused to see him. With Nate standing guard as her protector, there was little objection he could make. And Kit lingered in bed the third day just to avail herself of her grandfather's protection.

The fourth day she had little recourse except to resume her duties. But she was still weak and forced to limit the amount of work she did, depending on how strenuous it was.

It was inevitable that she would encounter Reese. He was by the barn talking to Frank when she rode in on her first afternoon out. Kit was too tired to try to avoid meeting him. She made no objection when he stepped forward to hold her horse's head while she dismounted.

"How are you, Kit?" he asked, leveling those hazel eyes at her.

"Fine," she lied.

"I stopped by to see how you were getting along, but Nate said you didn't want to see me."

"That's right." She hooked the stirrup onto the saddlehorn and began loosening the cinch.

"Did you need time to get firmly entrenched in your shell again?" Reese taunted. "Were you afraid if you kept seeing me while you recovered you might find you couldn't get back in?''

"Look, Reese," Kit began impatiently, "I'm tired. I'm really not up to one of your stupid discussions."

"I can see that." His sharp gaze skimmed over the faint pallor beneath her tan, brought there by weariness. "I should take advantage of it, since you wouldn't have the strength to put up too much of an argument. But I won't. Not this time, anyway," he declared and walked away to leave Kit trembling inwardly at his implied threat.

During the course of the following week she saw him many times. He always spoke, sometimes only a courteous greeting, other times inquiring about some facet of the ranch work. But his indifferent words didn't fool Kit. The look in his eyes told her that he hadn't forgotten a word he'd said and was simply biding his time.

It was a hot Sunday afternoon that found Kit prowling restlessly about the house. It was too hot to be doing any work. She could hear Lew and Frank out tinkering in the shed. Kyle had gone home for the day to visit his family and Mrs. Kent had the day off. Her grandfather was sitting by the window facing the ranch yard with a book in his lap. Kit saw him looking out and did the same through the panes of another window. Reese was riding the buckskin, leaving the yard, heading west. Some of the tension left Kit when he disappeared from sight.

"I think I'll go for a walk, Nate," she said, "down by the river. It should be cooler there."

"Okay."

They both knew the river was in the opposite direction from the one Reese took, but neither mentioned it. Before leaving the house Kit changed into a pair of cutoff jeans and sandals. They would be cooler than the heavy Levi's and she could easily slip her sandals off to wade in the shallow rapids at the bend in the river.

In the shade of the towering cottonwoods it was cooler. The ground had a thin coating of fluffy white seeds from which the trees had gotten their name. A slight breeze rustled the leaves, the sound nearly drowned by the laughing water of the rapids.

Kit waded for a while, leaving her sandals on the bank. When she got tired of that she sat on a water-smoothed boulder near the center of the river and dangled her feet in the water, letting the gentle rush cool her.

It was with reluctance, a sense of passing time and supper to be fixed, that she finally left her perch and waded back to the riverbank where she had left her shoes. There was no way to dry her feet so it took some doing to wedge them into the sandals. Eventually succeeding, Kit started back to the house. Her attention was on the ground, intent on not tripping over any of the many twigs and branches scattered about.

A horse snorted and Kit looked up, stopping

abruptly at the sight of Reese astride the buckskin at the edge of the trees. He had seen her and was waiting. Somehow she knew he had stopped waiting. This was the moment. To try to escape or avoid him would be useless because he would simply follow. Kit could only hope that she would be able to brazen her way through him.

"It's a crime against nature to cover up a pair of legs like yours in men's Levi's." Reese observed the length of her shapely legs as Kit walked closer.

His remark suddenly made her self-conscious of her skimpy—for her—attire. "How did you know I was down here?" she demanded.

"I was up on the ridge and caught a glimpse of a woman wading in the river." A wicked light danced in his eyes. "I knew it wasn't Mrs. Kent because her hair isn't that ripely golden brown color. By a process of elimination, it had to be you."

When Kit would have walked past him, Reese nudged the buckskin forward to block her path. "Come on." He extended a hand to her. "It's a long way up the hill to the house. I'll give you a ride."

But Kit didn't trust him to take her to the house and ducked under the horse's head. "No, thank you. I'd rather walk than accept a ride from you."

"Kit." There was a wealth of exasperation and impatience in the sighing way he said her name and the shake of his head. He reined the horse around to walk beside her. "It's hot and there's no sense wearing yourself out climbing that hill when you can ride.''

The house was out of sight, just beyond that slight rise. Kit stared fixedly in its direction, ignoring the bobbing head of the buckskin beside her. She walked briskly, feeling the pull on the muscles in the back of her legs at the steadily angling slope.

"I told you I'd rather walk," she repeated forcefully.

"You are going to ride." Reese leaned partially out of the saddle to hook an arm around her middle and scoop her off the ground, hauling her across the front of his saddle almost before Kit knew what was happening.

"Put me down!" She struggled and kicked and tried to slide out of his hold.

"What's the matter?" he taunted. "Don't you see us riding off into the sunset together?"

"Let me go!" Kit struck at him, but he easily pinned her arms to his sides.

"Have you noticed?" Reese emitted a throaty laugh. "You always are hissing and clawing before you start to purr, kitten."

"No," she gulped.

"Yes," he insisted.

Twisting her chin around, he captured her lips with forceful mastery. The crush of his arms locked Kit to his chest as the crazy, wild magic of his enchanting spell trapped her just as securely. His fingers slid through the brown silk of her hair, shaping the back of her head with his hand.

It was a soul-destroying kiss, setting free her inhibitions.

"You want me," Reese muttered thickly against her skin, "as much as I want you. Admit it, Kit. Put us both out of our misery and admit that you want me."

He was asking too much of her. She surfaced from an emotional tidal pool with a rush, realizing how quickly and easily her feelings could betray her pride.

"No. No! History isn't going to repeat itself. I am not going to be seduced by you!" Kit protested. Her arms strained against his chest, fighting for a single inch of space between them. "Put me down!"

Still holding her, Reese swung out of the saddle, stepping to the ground before setting her feet down. She would have run instantly, but his hands retained their hold on her shoulders, fingers cutting deeply into her soft flesh.

"Is that what you think you are running from? A simple seduction?" he accused cynically.

"What else do you call it?" Kit hurled. "You only want to amuse yourself with me. I'm just a plaything, a sexthing to you."

"I have more reasons for wanting you than solely for physical gratification, but we are getting off the subject," Reese snapped. "I'm talking about you and your reasons for running. You aren't running from me."

"No, I'm escaping!"

"From a fate worse than death?" he jeered.

"Yes. I'll never give in to you."

"Not because you are afraid of me. You are afraid of yourself." He took his hands from her as if his violence was so great he might do her bodily harm if he continued to hold her.

But his statement kept Kit from running to the safety of the house. "That is ridiculous," she denied it vigorously.

"A moment ago you spoke of history repeating itself."

She tossed her head back. "Have you forgotten? It way my mother who was seduced by the last baron. He wanted her, too, for the same, cheap, degrading reasons as you have."

"What's your opinion of your mother?" Reese demanded. "Do you think she was weak? Naive? Lacking in moral character? A coward?"

"It's pretty obvious, isn't it? I mean, she did let herself get taken in by all his fancy talk. She let him make love to her, didn't she?" It hurt to make those admissions about her mother, but they were the truth as Kit saw it. "She didn't stand up to him and say it was wrong."

"Your mother may have been misguided in placing her trust in him, but she had a hell of a lot more guts than you do!" he flared. "You are the one who is a coward, Kit."

"How can you say that? How can you accuse *me* of that?"

"Because you are afraid. Your mother cared

enough about a man to make a commitment to him, to have his child. She risked the shame and the hurt because she cared about a man. I can't believe your mother was stupid, weak or a coward. She knew what the consequences could be for her actions, but she did it anyway. I'm not saying it was right, but I'm betting that she did it with her eyes wide open, not blinded by a romantic dream."

"She was a fool!"

"No, you are the fool, Kit!" Reese seemed to loom above her in avenging anger, his face darkened, his arrogant nostrils flared, his mouth thinning into a forbidding line. "You don't have the guts to care. You're scared, scared to the bottom of your shoes! You pretend to be hard and tough to hide how petrified you are. You're a sniveling little coward."

"No, no, it's not true!" Kit covered her hands over her ears to shut out his hammering, hateful words.

Reese jerked them down. "Have you ever said 'I love you' to anything? To a dog, to a horse, to your grandfather? Have you said those words to anything or anybody? No," he answered the question for her. "No, because that would mean you cared. And if you cared you might get hurt."

"Let me go and leave me alone!" she cried.

"Gladly—on both counts!" He released her abruptly and Kit stumbled backward. "Run, Kit, run. That's all you know how to do, but stop kidding yourself and grow up!''

She took a few, faltering steps toward the house and stopped to hurl the last spear. ''Why don't you go away? Why don't you go away and never come back!''

He stood there glaring at her, his hands on his hips. Then he turned away and climbed into the saddle. With a flick of the reins, he spun the buckskin around and rode out toward the range. Kit ran a little farther up the hill, then collapsed in the tall grasses and started crying.

She pounded her fist into the ground, sobbing, ''I hate him. I hate him.'' Empty words without meaning and another way of running from the truth.

Kit was dry-eyed when she walked to the house much later. She didn't say a word to her grandfather about her meeting with Reese.

Two days later Kit was stepping out of the barn after milking the cow when she saw Reese's car parked in front of the Big House. Puzzled, she stared. That wasn't where it belonged. Her frown deepened as Reese walked out, dressed in a suit and carrying two large pieces of luggage.

Her heart started pounding like a death drum. Slowly, drawn like a metal to magnet, Kit crossed the yard and approached the car. Reese was stowing the luggage in the rear compartment of the car. He didn't even glance up when she stopped by the front fender, milk bucket in hand.

The housekeeper came bustling out of the house onto the porch. "You forgot your shaving kit, Mr. Talbot." She started down the steps, holding out a small, brown leather case. She spied Kit standing by the car and stopped on the last step, glancing uncertainly toward Reese.

"Thank you, Mrs. Kent." He took the shaving kit from her, still without so much as a glance to acknowledge Kit's presence. "I appreciate your staying on another couple of days to close things up. Lew or Frank will take you into town whenever you're ready to leave."

Close things up! The phrase struck Kit like a slap across the face. That sounded much more permanent than a simple trip.

"I don't mind." The woman hesitated, then added, "I enjoyed working for you, Mr. Talbot, truly I did."

"Goodbye, Mrs. Kent." Reese shook her hand and gave her a smile that had grim edges to it, as did his features.

"Goodbye, sir." There was a slight catch in the woman's voice. She cast one last, spurious glance at Kit and walked back up the steps into the house.

Still Reese ignored her, carrying the shaving kit to the rear of the car and tossing it in the trunk with the rest of his luggage.

"You're leaving," she finally blurted out the words.

"Yes." Reese slammed the lid of the trunk down.

"For good?"

"Yes." He walked to the passenger door, opened it, and started to slide behind the wheel.

She caught at the door to keep him from closing it. Reese finally looked at her, one foot resting inside the car, his face closed, revealing nothing.

"Without even saying goodbye?"

"I thought we'd said our goodbyes," he answered coldly.

"I—" What could she say? He was so aloof, so cool. Kit shuddered and looked away.

"How does it feel, Kit?" he taunted.

"What?" Her voice was small, no more than a thread of a sound. There were tears at the back of her eyes, stinging and smarting.

"You won. I'm leaving and you're staying," Reese elaborated. "How does it feel to get what you want?"

"I—don't know." She stared at him, searching those impenetrable male features.

"It is what you wanted, isn't it?" A brow arched, arrogant and mocking.

"Yes," Kit breathed in agreement, but the past tense was the operative thing. It was what she had wanted. Only now. . . . She had never believed he would leave.

His mouth curved in an unfriendly smile. "I hope you enjoy your victory celebration." He started again to climb into the car, tossing an idly cutting, "Have a drink for me."

"Why?" Kit forestalled him again.

"Why what?" That bland yet piercing gaze was on her again.

"Why are you leaving?"

"Because of you." There was a cynical, almost bitter twist of his mouth. "To borrow a cliché from an old Western movie—this place isn't big enough for both of us."

"And you're leaving," Kit repeated what she found so difficult to accept.

"It has to be me," Reese informed her. "You couldn't survive anywhere else. There wouldn't be any place you could hide."

Kit flinched at his words, as he had meant her to. "You don't have to go."

"Don't I?" He laughed. "It doesn't matter. I want to go."

"You do?" That hurt more than anything he could have said. If she had felt she had driven him away it would have been easier somehow. But to have him want to leave... Kit found that painful.

"I've discovered that I prefer women who wear dresses once in a while instead of running around all the time in men's clothes. When I hold another woman in my arms, her skin will smell of perfume instead of horse sweat, manure and hay. Her hair will be styled in the latest fashion and not jammed under some dirty hat. She won't have a chip on her shoulder, running around daring everyone to knock it off, and she won't swear like a cowboy."

Each sentence sliced across her like the biting lash of a bullwhip, cutting to the bone. Kit felt driven to the ground. She was surprised to discover she was still standing upright without a mark on her.

Reese wasn't finished. "She won't be afraid to be a woman. She won't be afraid to be human."

Kit let go of the door and stepped away. Every centimeter of her body felt pain, so intense that it numbed her. Her face felt frozen as she looked at him.

"Goodbye."

He gripped the door for a taut second, then slipped behind the wheel and slammed it shut. The motor roared to life and the tires spun once before acquiring traction. Kit watched him drive out of the yard until the dust settled.

CHAPTER NINE

DAZED BY AN EVENT she was not prepared for, Kit walked blindly to her house. As if a robot programmed to perform a certain routine, she walked into the kitchen, strained the milk from the pail into a pitcher and set it in the refrigerator. She rinsed out the pail and set it on the porch. When she turned, her grandfather was standing in the living room archway, staring at her stricken expression.

"Reese has gone," she said.

"I know," he nodded quietly.

"He isn't coming back," Kit added.

"I know."

"How? When?" The numbness was beginning to wear off and a million needle-sharp pains began stabbing her. It wasn't right that Nate had known and not told her.

"He came over this morning and told me," Nate explained.

"He wasn't going to tell me," Kit murmured with a faint sob in her voice. "He was just going to leave. If I hadn't seen him—" The lump in her throat choked off the rest of the sentence.

"It took me by surprise, too, Kitty." He seemed to be attempting to console her.

"Did he—" Kit hardly dared to hope "—did he ask you to tell me anything?" Perhaps he hadn't planned to leave without giving her a message of some sort. Although why she thought so after his barrage of barbed insults, Kit didn't know.

"He—" Nate hesitated, then shook his head sadly. "He didn't mention you at all."

"Oh." The world was beginning to shatter. If Reese could see her now he wouldn't find any chip on her shoulder.

"You didn't want him to go, did you, child?" he asked gently.

"No." Huge and round, her eyes were brimming with tears, large brown pools of misery. "He was right about me, Nate. He said I was afraid to care. He said I kept running from people, shutting them out because I was afraid to have them close in case they hurt me. And it's true, Nate," she sobbed and tried to smile. "I'm afraid of being a woman. I'm afraid of having feelings that any normal human being has."

"Oh, Kit, Kit." His sad voice seemed to take on some of her pain. He moved toward her and she crossed the space to wrap her arms around him and bury her face in his shirt, the tears spilling over her lashes.

"Do you know—" Kit laughed bitterly through her tears "—I don't think I've ever told you that I love you, grandpa."

"You didn't have to," he assured her. "I've always known it."

"I should have said it."

"There, there, child." He patted her head and rocked her gently in his arms.

"I love him, grandpa." She told him what in her heart she had longed to tell him. Now that Reese had unlocked her shell and thrown away the key, all her troubled thoughts and feelings came pouring out.

"I've known that, too," Nate murmured.

"What Reese told you is true, grandpa." Unconsciously she wasn't even using his given name any longer. "Nothing happened. He kissed me, but he never made love to me."

"I believe you."

"He wanted to, but I kept running away. I wish I hadn't now." She tipped her tear-drenched face back to look up at his lined features. "Isn't the awful? I wish he had made love to me. I wish I was going to have his baby. Then I would have something of him to love now that he's gone. I want it so much it hurts."

A sharp pain flashed across his face and he trembled. "You sound just like your mother, Kitty. That's almost exactly what Sara said to me."

"She...she wanted to have me?" Kit wiped the dampness from her cheek with the back of her hand, sniffling a bit as she tried to find control.

"Oh, gracious, yes, child." Nate smiled. This

time there was a shimmer of tears in his eyes. "Whatever made you think that she didn't?"

"I . . . don't know. I thought maybe she resented me because I was there to remind her of what had happened," Kit explained hesitantly. "She certainly couldn't forget it with me around."

"Sara loved you. She loved you even before you were born. And afterwards—" his smile broadened "—she wouldn't let you out of her sight. Always holding you and talking to you and watching you sleep. She spent practically every minute with you just as if—" his voice faded slightly "—just as if she knew she wouldn't have much time with you."

"What happened? You and grandma told me that she died of pneumonia, but I always wondered. . . . Was that it?" she asked, then saw how sad he looked and added, "Do you mind talking about it?"

"No." He stroked her hair, brushing it away where it tried to cling to her damp cheek. "We probably should have done it before. But Martha and me, we told you when you were a child what we felt you should know then. We thought when you grew up, if you had any more questions, you would ask. When you didn't, we thought it best to leave it alone."

"I'd like to know about—momma."

"She did die of pneumonia. That was true," he began. "Sara never did recover like she should have after having you. When she got sick, well, she just never had the strength to fight it off."

"And I thought that she didn't want to live," Kit murmured to herself, "that she was too ashamed."

"No, she wanted to see you grow into a beautiful woman. She wanted to live, all right, but it just wasn't to be. I know she didn't want to leave you."

"If she saw me now I have the feeling she would be disappointed," Kit sighed.

"I don't think so. You've had more of a burden to carry than most. I think she'd understand if you took the wrong path for a while. She wasn't perfect, either."

"My father—the baron—did she hate him after the way he had treated her? Or did she still love him?" she questioned.

"Sara loved him. She fell in love with him the first minute she laid eyes on him. She found out almost at the beginning that he was married, but she never told Martha and me. That didn't stop her. She knew she could never marry him. The baron's wife was an invalid, I guess, and divorce was unheard of in his family anyway." He paused. "Later Sara told us that she decided if she couldn't have the baron, she'd have his child. She wanted something of him she could love when he was gone." Nate pressed a kiss to Kit's forehead. "Do you see what I meant earlier? You said almost exactly the same thing."

But Kit was thinking how right Reese had been about her mother. There had been nothing naive or stupid or weak about what she had done. Her eyes had been open, perhaps with just a touch of romantic haze, though.

"And the baron? Did he love my mother?" She had learned so much that she couldn't help wondering if there was more.

"He told Sara he loved her, but I can't say whether he actually meant it or whether he said it just to have his way with her. Although sometimes I've wondered whether your mother would have cared or not if he did."

Kit rested her head against his shoulder. "Maybe he did," she murmured. "Maybe he cared a little." For the first time in her life she was willing to give the baron the benefit of the doubt.

"Maybe."

Liquid pain shot through her veins. "What am I going to do, grandpa? Reese said he wasn't coming back."

"I know, child. I know," Nate comforted.

"Did he mean it? Won't I ever see him again?" Kit whispered, terrified by the thought and all its wretched implications.

"I don't know." She felt the shake of his head, then heard his sigh. "I'm sorry, Kitty, but he doesn't strike me as the type to say something he doesn't mean."

And Reese had said he was leaving for good. Kit began crying for her blindness, her stupidity, her cowardice, for the loss of something she hadn't known she'd found until it was gone. The years behind that shell had dammed up a lake of tears. They were all released in one giant emotional purging.

Her grandfather held her closely in his arms with loving unconcern for the drenching of his shirt. Eventually there were no tears left and Kit's sobs were reduced to dry, hiccuping sounds.

"Dry your eyes, child," Nate insisted, pressing his handkerchief into her hand. "I know you want to go on crying forever, but you can't." He loosened his hold and let an arm curve around her shoulders. "Come over here and sit down. I'll pour you a cup of coffee. How's that sound?"

Kit nodded an acceptance, blowing her nose and wiping the briny taste from her lips while he guided her to a kitchen chair, but she really didn't care about the coffee. She didn't care about anything.

Nate Bonner, in his wisdom, sensed that. He set the coffee before her and took another chair from the table, drawing it alongside of Kit. "You think life isn't worth going on without him, don't you?"

"Yes," she sniffed, winding her shaking hands around the hot coffee.

"You'll find a reason," he promised. "At first, you might only get up in the mornings to milk the cow. Later it might be to see the fall roundup through. In time there'll be a reason."

Kit shook her head, not believing it was possible to be true, not the way she felt, despite the conviction in his voice. "I don't—" she started to deny it, then it hit her. "You know, don't you? You must have felt worse than this when grandma died." He'd had all those years of loving his wife and Kit had known love only such a short time.

"When Martha left, all my reason for going on went with her," Nate admitted. "At least that's what I thought. But I was wrong. You needed me yet. Nothing happens without a purpose, Kitty. I believe that."

But where was hers? "I hope you're right, grandpa," she murmured, staring into the black liquid in the mug and wishing she could drown in it.

"Drink up, child," he urged, and Kit obediently lifted the mug to her mouth.

IN THE BEGINNING it was as her grandfather had predicted. Life didn't seem worth living without Reese. When Kit would wake in the mornings the ponderous weight of her heartache would come crushing down on her. Her only desire was to roll over and curl into a tight ball of misery, but she would hear the milk cow bellowing up by the barn and drag herself out of bed.

There was no bitterness, only pain that racked her body and her heart. Minute by minute Kit got through each day. Half the time she didn't know what she was doing. She went through the motions of living, initially for her grandfather's sake and later because it was the thing to do.

The worst times were when she sent in the monthly reports and accounts to the office of the attorney whose address Reese had given them after his inheritance, before she had ever met him. Kit wondered if Reese ever saw them. What checks that came were from the ranch account with some stranger's signature affixed to them.

July rolled into August. August became September and Kit's spirit began to heal. Subconsciously a purpose entered her life. Reese's parting words sparked a series of concessions by Kit to her sex. The hardness, the toughness, he had taken with him when he left. There was no mask on her features to hide her feelings.

The men's shirts were abandoned. Those that were still in good condition Kit gave to charity. The rest were thrown in the rag bag. New blouses were purchased, darted and tailored to accent the roundness of her breasts and the slender curve of her waist. Worn and patched men's Levi's suffered the same fate as the men's shirts. A streak of practicality kept Kit from throwing all of them out, but she supplemented her supply of denims with ones that snuggly fitted her rounded figure instead of bagging at the seat.

Her stained, brown Stetson hat was burned and a new one was bought. It was a cream white straw cowboy hat with a shallower crown. There was no room inside it to pile her long hair. When she rode now, her chestnut gold hair either swung about her shoulders or was caught by a barrette at the nape of her neck.

There were two new dresses hanging in her

closet, the old, outdated ones from her school days taking the charity route. There was a bottle of perfume on her dresser, and eye shadow, mascara and lipstick.

Always there was the silent strength flowing from her grandfather to Kit. Eventually she wanted to show her appreciation for his unwavering support and understanding. Kit began to take more interest in the housework.

Her grandmother had been meticulous about her home, always wanting it to look its best. Previously Kit's version had been a lick and a promise and she thought her grandfather might be missing the pride his wife had taken. Kit discovered that cooking and cleaning weren't quite the drudgery she had thought. There was a challenging aspect to it that she needed, although she still enjoyed actual ranch work more.

Along with everything else, Kit began going into town more often. Without that cold, hardened reserve of aloofness, more people greeted her on the street. Kit even began to speak first to familiar faces of neighbors and acquaintances. They remarked among themselves about her new friendliness, commented on how attractive she seemed and speculated about the haunting sadness that lurked in her eyes. Those who knew about Reese and his sudden departure and had heard the rumors about the possible affair between them drew their own conclusions.

Kit no longer bristled when she received sympathetic looks. She was amazed by the fact that others might care how she felt. She accepted their sympathy without comment, but kept the privacy of her loss to herself.

She never stopped missing Reese, or regretting, or wanting him. Every hour of every day, Kit ached for him. At times it was just a dull ache. Others, it was a sharp, searing pain that stabbed at her heart like a hot knife. She didn't expect it would change for a very long time, if ever, but Kit accepted that. As much as anyone can be, Kit was reconciled to her life.

Bacon sizzled in the skillet, brown and crisp. Kit scooped it out and spread it across a plate covered with a paper towel to drain. She turned as her grandfather entered the kitchen, and smiled.

"Good morning."

"Morning." He looked tired and his thatch of white hair was still touseled from sleep. "It's a bit nippy out this morning."

"Downright chilly." Kit broke two eggs in the skillet of hot bacon fat.

Outside there was a honking sound and Nate Bonner peered out a slightly steamed-over window to see the V-formation of a flock of migrating geese winging their way south.

"Winter's coming for sure," he sighed. "I guess I'd better get the Big House shuttered and all checked out for winter while the decent weather is still holding."

There was a sharp stab in her midsection and

Kit said, "Yes, you'd probably better." She flipped the eggs over with a spatula.

"Are you going out with the boys this morning?" Nate inquired, tactfully changing the subject.

"Yes. We should get the last of the cows up to the winter pasture today." Kit slid his fried eggs onto a plate, setting it and the platter of bacon on the table in front of him. She turned back to the stove to crack an egg in the skillet for herself.

"Be cold riding today," he observed as he reached for the bread just popping out of the toaster.

"I'm wearing my thermal underwear just in case you're right." Kit smiled.

"It shows," Nate murmured dryly.

Kit glanced down at her tapered blouse and snug Levi's. With the heavy long underwear beneath them the pants were almost skintight.

"It does bulge a bit," she admitted with a faint laugh. "But I'll keep warm."

"So you figure you'll finish up today?" Nate reverted back to the subject of the day's ranch work.

Kit continued to give most of the orders, but she no longer dictated. In the first numbed weeks after Reese had left, all three of the hands had been quite gentle with her. Since then, a pleasant camaraderie had developed among them. And Kit wouldn't have gone back to her old ways and destroy this new relationship for anything.

"Yes, we should," she answered in response to his comment. "It'll probably be late though. I didn't think Frank would feel much like cooking when we got back so I'm going to invite them over for supper. There's a big pot of chili at the back of the stove, roast beef sandwiches and a couple of salads in the refrigerator. That should satisfy them, don't you think?"

"Should," he agreed. There was a twinkle in his eye when Kit dished up her egg and sat down beside him. "Especially with the chocolate cake you've got hiding in the cupboard for dessert."

"You found it," she accused.

"Tasted pretty good, too."

"Is there any left?"

"Enough for dessert tonight and a snack for me this afternoon," her grandfather said with a wink.

"You and that sweet tooth of yours are hopeless," Kit declared.

"You'd better eat. Your egg's getting cold," he warned. "Want some toast?"

"Please."

"And don't be riding me about my sweet tooth," Nate added. "Yours is just as bad."

Her knifeful of butter was poised just above the piece of toast in her hand. Unwittingly, her grandfather had reminded her of that time when Reese had mocked her sweet craving of the French-fried vanilla ice cream dessert. Kit waited for the sharp pang to subside, then buttered her toast.

CHAPTER TEN

FROST HAD ALREADY TURNED the tall, thick grass into a swaying carpet of tawny gold. The rugged grandeur of the land did not display spectacular autumn plumage. There were only the rusty oranges and yellows of the tree leaves along the watercourses to contrast with the dark green of juniper-covered slopes. As a rule fall days were mild and the nights chilly, giving the animals, ranch stock and wildlife alike, a chance to grow winter coats.

Today it had been decidedly brisk with a bite to the wind. A startling blue sky stretched endlessly overhead. The sun was on its swift downward path, shortening the hours of daylight. Winter came early to the badlands, the first snowflurries coming sometimes as soon as late September. They were approaching that time and the air held a warning of winter's cold breath not far away.

A quartet of horses and riders plodded along the dirt track toward the ranch yard. They crested a hill and Kit glimpsed the roof of the Big House through the windbreak of trees. There was a constriction in her chest as she again found it hard to accept that Reese would never walk within its walls again.

"Man, I ain't never been so tired and sore in all my life," Kyle moaned, wincing as he tried to shift in the saddle. "My butt's really going to be dragging tonight."

Kit mentally shook away her previous thoughts of Reese. "Come on, Kyle," she chided. "You've been sitting on it all day." There was a time when she would have snapped at Kyle for complaining instead of teasing him.

"That's the point," he groaned and the others laughed sympathetically, aware of their own stiffened muscles from their long day in the saddle.

"What you need is some hard riding to loosen you up. Come on. I'll race you to the barn," Kit challenged, suddenly wanting to hear the wind singing in her ears and stop its whispering of Reese's name in the grasses.

Before Kyle could accept or reject her challenge, Kit was putting the spurs to the bay. She had a two-stride head start before Kyle gave chase. Both horses flattened out, glad to race as long as they were headed for the barn and oats. Kyle was never able to close the gap. When they reined in at the barn Kit was the victor.

"You won," he conceded, "but only because you had a head start."

His hand was at her waist to help her down. The action recalled for Kit another time when Reese's hands had forcibly helped her from the saddle, the time of their first kiss.

She swallowed the lump in her throat and attempted a light retort. "Your horse has always been faster than Reno. I won because I was the better rider." She hopped to the ground with his friendly assistance.

"I admit you have the prettiest seat in a saddle that I've ever seen," Kyle said, letting his hand fall away now that she was standing.

His comment astonished Kit. He was actually flirting with her, not in any serious way, but in the light, teasing vein of a man who finds a woman attractive and wants her to know it.

"I'll take care of your horse," he offered.

She no longer regarded such offers as a slur that she was the weaker sex and therefore incapable. Instead of strongly objecting, Kit handed him the reins.

"Thanks," she said and Kyle left, leading both horses into the corral.

As she turned to leave the barn area, she discovered Lew and Frank had ridden up behind her. Lew had dismounted and Frank was leading both horses away. Kit could tell by the bright glitter in Lew's eyes that he had overheard Kyle's comment.

"He was actually flirting with me. Can you believe that?" She laughed out some of her amazement.

"I can believe it," he nodded. "You have changed, Kitty. I can remember when a comment like that would have earned a fella twenty lashes or the equivalent thereof from your sharp tongue. It's dulled considerably.''

"I guess it has.'' Looking into his weather-tanned face, Kit knew she had never been properly appreciative of this man's unwavering loyalty and affection. He was more like an uncle she had never had. "Thanks for being so patient and tolerant, Lew.'' Impulsively, Kit leaned up and kissed his scratchy cheek.

"For cryin' out loud!'' He flushed a deep red. "What ya going' an' gettin' all mushy for?'' Behind the embarrassment there was a profoundly touched look and Kit knew she would have done it again, given the chance.

Instead she laughed, "That's what you get for having a woman boss.'' She walked past him, giving him a pat on the rump, a male gesture that she copied in fun and Lew sidestepped quickly in deeper embarrassment.

"Behave yourself!'' he admonished.

Turning around, Kit continued to walk backward. Her laughing gaze accidentally caught sight of the Big House and the front door standing open. Momentarily her heart gave a leap, but she quieted it, speaking aloud the explanation.

"It looks like gramps is still up at the Big House getting it ready for winter. I'm going to see how he's coming along,'' she informed Lew unnecessarily. "Don't forget—supper will be ready in forty-five minutes, give or take.''

"Don't burn it," he warned.

"I won't." Kit changed directions and started for the Big House.

The warming events of the last few minutes lightened her steps as she crossed the yard. Kit concentrated her thoughts on those, letting the pain of Reese throb at the back of her mind. There was only silence when she set foot inside the house.

"Grandpa? Nate?" she called and received no answer.

But she thought she heard a sound of someone moving about in the rear of the house. After a second's hesitation Kit went to investigate. The library door was closed and she walked past it, deliberately not looking at it. It was still the only room in the house that Kit couldn't face.

Dustcovers were draped over the furniture in the parlor-type living room. Thankfully the windows to the west were unshuttered, letting the sunlight stream in to chase away the gloom. Kit glimpsed a movement out of the corner of her eye when she entered the room and stopped. It was only her own reflection in the big oval mirror on the wall, encircled by a polished and ornately carved hardwood frame.

The sight of herself in the mirror caused her to pause. The blouse and the Levi's molded her well-shaped but not overly rounded figure, but there could be little doubt that she was a woman. Her hair curled easily about her shoulders, a little

tousled by the wind, the gleam of golden sunlight
in its brown depths. The proud, defensive look
was gone from her features, her lips softened into
curves instead of pulled thin.

Kit wondered if Reese would notice the changes
if he saw her now. Would things have turned out
differently if she had looked like this when they
had met? But she would never know the answer to
either of those questions.

His image joined her reflection in the mirror. She blinked and stared at the hard-cut features with their brooding, aristocratic air, that
glint of mockery in the piercing hazel eyes, the
cruelly sensuous mouth and that crisply waving
dark hair.

No matter how much she willed the haunting
image to go away, it remained. Then it moved
toward her. Kit went white and pivoted to face it.
Reese was standing there—in the flesh.

"Hello, Kit," he said in the low, quiet voice she
remembered so well.

"I thought you were a ghost," she breathed.

His mouth quirked in a half-smiling line. "I was
surprised by what I saw, too."

"You're back," Kit said. Though why she had
to say it when it was so obvious, she didn't know.

"Yes, I'm back."

A warm glow seemed to flood through her
body, a treacherous joy leaping in her heart. Once
she would have demanded to know why he was
back, but the change in Kit had produced a reti-

cence that kept her from asking what had brought him back.

"When. . . did you get here?" she asked.

"This afternoon. About an hour ago," Reese answered.

There was not that much distance separating them. One step and Kit could be in his arms, but she didn't attempt to cross it. Not yet. It was too soon. He might still despise her and Kit couldn't endure it if he rejected her. His expression was impenetrable and she didn't know what he thought of her now.

"You've changed, Kit," he said, his gaze raking her figure.

So he had noticed, she thought breathlessly. And did he know why?

"Yes," Kit agreed, "although—" she lifted her arm to sniff the back of her hand, then smiled "—I still smell of horse sweat and manure."

When she would have dropped her hand, Reese caught it and carried it up to his nose, his breath warm against her skin. His gaze continued to hold Kit's over her hand. "And a trace of perfume," he added, lowering her hand and slowly releasing it. There was something questioning in the way he studied her face. "You are more beautiful than I remembered."

"I—I'm glad you think so." The words sounded so inadequate when the cup of her happiness was spilling over inside. "How long will you be staying, Reese?"

"That depends." But he didn't say on what. "I'm afraid I came unannounced again," he offered wryly. "Do you suppose Frank can stretch the evening meal to include me again?"

"I'm sure he can. No...." Quickly Kit retracted her answer. In the surprise of seeing Reese again she had forgotten. "I invited the boys over to the house to eat with grandpa and me. So Frank isn't cooking."

"I can drive into town and get something to eat then."

"No, please join us," she invited hurriedly. "There's plenty of food, honestly."

"I'd like that," he agreed. His gaze sharpened as he noticed the way Kit practically radiated with boundless joy. "I saw you when you rode into the yard this afternoon, laughing and joking with the others," Reese mused. "I could hardly believe you were the same Kit."

"I suppose you could say I've mellowed with age," she suggested.

"Yes, you have grown up." He tipped his head to the side in an inquiring angle. "Did a man have anything to do with it?"

Was he uncertain of her? "Oh, yes, definitely," Kit answered.

An eyebrow lifted. "Anyone I know?"

A smile beamed on her face. "You know him very well. It's—" The "you" part of the sentence never got out of her mouth.

"Kit?" a voice called from the hallway, and

both of them turned at the interruption. "Hey, Kit? Are you in here?" A second later Kyle appeared. Reese was standing slightly to one side so it was Kit he was first. "You left your jacket tied on the back of your saddle. Lew told me you were in here so I thought I'd better bring it to you before you started wondering where it was."

"Thanks, Kyle." She reached out for the leather-fringed jacket he was carrying.

But Kyle had stopped short at the sight of Reese. A look of stunned surprise was replaced by a wide grin of welcome. "Mr. Talbot! Wow! I didn't expect to see you here." Vigorously he shook Reese's hand. "This is quite a surprise. When did you get back?"

"A while ago."

Kit heard the sudden note of reserve in Reese's voice and stared at him. He did seem withdrawn, with a chilling hardness about his expression. It frightened her, especially the way he avoided looking at her.

Maybe he had guessed what she was going to say before Kyle had come in and was glad she hadn't had the chance. What made her think he might have come back because of her? Because that was what she wanted to believe, Kit realized.

It was more than likely he had returned on ranch business. Perhaps he had decided to sell after all and be done with any connection to her for good. It was a restraining thought, one that put a curb on her riotous joy.

"This is really something else!" Kyle declared with an amazed shake of his head. "Wait until the others hear. It's good to have you back, sir."

"Thanks." Reese's mouth curved, but it wasn't a smile.

Kyle suddenly realized he was still holding Kit's jacket. He turned to give it to her, his gaze lighting on her slightly pale complexion. His expression immediately sobered as he glanced warily back to Reese.

"Was I...interrupting something?" he asked in half challenge, not sure if Kit needed or wanted his protection.

"No," Reese answered, giving Kit the impression that he had no further desire to be alone with her. "Kit was just inviting me to join you all for dinner." Finally he looked at her, his gaze bland and unrevealing. "I have a few things to unpack yet. What time would you like me to come over?" So polite, so formal.

"We'll probably eat in half and hour or so. Anytime between now and then will be fine," Kit answered, telling herself not to be so disappointed.

Depending on how long he was staying, she might still have a chance. He had found her attractive once and he had just said she was more beautiful than he remembered. Surely there was hope in that.

"Good. I'll see you shortly, then," Reese nodded crisply.

With Kyle walking beside her, Kit left the house. She felt him eyeing her curiously, wondering what had gone on between them before he arrived, but he didn't ask and she didn't answer. Once outside the house he walked with her a little ways before parting to go to the bunkhouse and wash up before the meal.

Although Reese's return had not gone the way Kit had thought it might there for a while, the fact that he had come back at all was sufficient to ease the pain in her heart for the time being. She was smiling as she swept into the kitchen of her own home.

Her grandfather was standing at the stove. He glanced up when she entered. "You saw him, did you?" Nate said, certain of her positive answer.

"Yes." She rushed over to the stove and gave him a quick hug. "He's coming to dinner."

He smiled at the happiness sparkling in her brown eyes. "I put the chili on to heat when I saw you ride into the yard. The table is all set. I figured you'd invite him to dinner and I thought you might want a chance to maybe shower and put on a bit of lipstick."

"Grandpa, you are a love!" Kit declared with a laugh and dashed off to do just that.

Kit didn't take too much time because she didn't have long before Reese and the others came. Out of the shower, she toyed with the idea of wearing one of her new dresses, but decided that was too obvious. Dressed in dark blue denims and a flowered blouse, she reentered the kitchen. The chili was just beginning to simmer in its pot and Kit took the spoon away from her grandfather to stir it.

"Did Reese say anything to you about why he'd come back?" she asked.

"Nope. Did he to you?" Nate countered.

Kit shook her head but didn't have the chance to make a verbal answer as several pair of boots clomped onto the porch and the back door opened. She glanced up to see Frank walk in, followed by Lew and it looked like Kyle behind him.

"I'll have the food on the table in a few minutes," she promised, turning back to the chili. "Why don't you boys have a chair in the living room until I'm ready?"

As they started to file through to the living room, Lew teased, "Did you burn it?"

"No, I didn't," she retorted.

When Kit looked up, she saw that as well as all three ranch hands, Reese had arrived, too. He met her glance briefly and followed the others into the living room, her grandfather joining them and leaving the kitchen in Kit's domain.

A little nervous, Kit took the salads from the refrigerator and started taking them out of their plastic bag to arrange them on the platter. She tensed at the sound of footsteps in the kitchen. When she glanced over her shoulder, Kit saw it was Lew and relaxed.

"How's it goin'?" He leaned against the counter beside her, his astute gaze studying her downcast face.

"Fine. Be ready in a few minutes."

Lew watched her setting out the sandwiches for a few seconds, then asked, "Did he say why he's come back?"

"No." Kit shook her head briefly.

"Do you want me to have a little talk with him?" Lew frowned instantly. "I don't want to see you gettin' hurt by him again."

"No, there's no need," Kit answered, touched by his gallant gesture.

"Do ya' still love him?" He lowered his head to peer more closely at her face, revealing his shiny bald top.

"Yes, I do." She smiled wryly and set the last sandwich on the platter.

Kit picked it up and turned to carry it to the table. Reese was standing behind them, listening. She almost dropped the platter, but his hand was there to save it and set it on the table.

Reese turned back to her and demanded, "Who was that man you were referring to?"

There wasn't any point in holding back now, but Kit was shaking inside. "You."

In the next second his arms were around her and she was crushed to his chest. His mouth came down hard on her lips, bruising and punishing and loving with an ardor that took Kit's breath away. She strained to be closer to him, arching against his granite length, abandoning all restraint to respond to his possessive kiss. Hungrily they sought to ease the frustration of longing their separation had born in each of them. It couldn't be done in one passionate kiss.

Finally Reese cupped his hands on either side of her face and reluctantly took his mouth from hers. Desire smoldered in his eyes as he stared into the rapturous wonder of hers.

"Why did you come back?" Kit asked in a husky voice, now that she was sure of his answer.

"Because of you. I couldn't get you out of my head. Hell!" he chuckled, "I couldn't get you out of my heart."

"I love you, Reese." Kit spoke the words she had lived with so long, her heart pouring out its love.

He kissed her again and would have gone on kissing her, regardless of Lew's onlooker status. But it was Kyle's voice, out of sight of them in the living room, that made them both aware of the absence of their privacy.

"Hey! Out there in the kitchen! When are we going to eat? I'm starved!"

Kit blushed as she looked at Reese through the sweep of her lashes. His adoring and possessive smile made her swell with joy. He loved her and nothing could be more perfect than that. He curved an arm around her shoulder, nestling Kit against his side as he turned her toward the living room.

"Come with me," he ordered.

The others stopped talking the minute they entered the living room. Kit's color was still high, but she thought she would burst with her love. She couldn't have hidden it if her life depended on it. The whole world could know for all she cared.

Reese stopped in front of her grandfather. "With your permission, I'd like to marry your granddaughter."

Tears of pure ecstasy shimmered in her eyes as she looked up to him, hardly daring to believe she had heard correctly. It was a dream, a bliss-filled dream. But the look in his eyes told her she was wide-awake.

"I don't need to ask Kitty if it's what she wants," Nate replied, "because I know you've just made her the happiest woman on earth. You have my permission. And God bless you both."

His voice was husky with emotion. Kit had come to know her grandfather and she knew he was deeply moved because of the happiness this moment had brought her.

It seemed to take several seconds for what was happening to sink in with the others. When it did, there was an explosion of jubilation, back-slapping and congratulations passed all around. It was several minutes before Lew, who had joined them in the living room, thought to rescue the chili from the fire on the stove.

Their thoughts turned to food and the hunger they had temporarily forgotten. As they moved en masse into the kitchen, Reese caught at Kit's hand and dragged her away from the table toward the back door.

"If you'll excuse us for a few minutes?" he requested with a broad smile. "We'll join you later."

"It's cold outside. You'd better wear a coat," Nate cautioned.

As she and Reese started out the door, Kit saw Lew poke Frank in the ribs and mutter, "It could be freezing and they'd never know the difference."

Outside Kit found out how right Lew was. In Reese's arms the fire of their love was more than enough to keep both of them uncomfortably warm. It was a long while before either found the time or the necessity for words.

"I thought you wouldn't come back," Kit breathed finally as he cradled her head against his shoulders.

"I couldn't stay away any longer. I had to take another chance that I could get through that shell of yours," he said.

"It's gone."

"I noticed. In fact it was the first thing I noticed when I saw you out in the yard with Kyle. I had the terrible feeling that another man had wakened you while I was gone." His arms tightened around her, fiercely possessive. "When I asked you if there was a man, I assumed you meant someone else. Then Kyle walked in."

"And you thought it was him?" Kit couldn't believe it. He had been jealous.

"I wanted to tear him apart," Reese admitted.

"It was always you," she vowed. "There was never anyone else but you."

"I love you so much, Kit." He rubbed his chin against her hair, trembling with his need. "We'll be married right away."

"Yes," she agreed and caressed the tanned column of his throat. Peering up at him, Kit asked, "Where will we live when we're married?" She remembered how he had denied ever wanting a home.

"In the Big House. Will that suit you?"

"Here?" She raised her head to see if he was teasing her. "Do you mean we're going to live here? On the ranch?"

"Yes," Reese smiled at her amazement. "Do you want to?"

"Oh, yes, I want to," she said in a rush, then hesitated. "But do you?"

"I missed it," he said, and looked out at the western sun crimsoning the ragged bluffs. "As a matter of fact that's what brought me back. I knew you were still here and I decided if I couldn't beat you, I'd join you. So I decided to come back and marry you. I missed this place more than I missed you."

Tears stung her eyes as she stiffened in his arms, murmuring a cool, "I see."

He caught her chin and twisted it up to see her face. "That was a joke, kitten."

"Was it?" Kit wasn't quite sure.

"I missed this place, but not as much as I missed you. I love you," Reese assured her. "And as for marrying you just to live here, you are forgetting I own it."

Relief sighed in her throat and she relaxed against him. "I've become sensitive, I guess." She tried to explain. "I don't have anything to protect me anymore." She was referring to the shell she had always hidden behind.

"You have me, kitten," he promised.

That was more than enough.